Praise for *Pierrot Mon Ami*

"We always feel good reading a Queneau novel; he is the least depressing of the moderns, the least heavy, with something Mozartian about the easy, self-pleasing flow of his absurd plots."
—John Updike, *New Yorker*

"Wondrous."—Bill Marx, *Boston Phoenix*

"Raymond Queneau's books are ambiguous fairylands in which scenes of everyday life are mingled with a melancholy that is ageless. Though they are not without bitterness, their author seems always to set his face against conclusions, and to be moved by a kind of horror of seriousness. 'Foolishness,' according to Flaubert, 'consists of wanting to reach a conclusion.' One can imagine those words as the epigraph to Queneau's *Pierrot Mon Ami*."
—Albert Camus

"A comic masterpiece."—Irving Malin, *Hollins Critic*

"A carnival ride of surprises and pleasures."—*Kirkus Reviews*

Other Books by Raymond Queneau in English Translation

Raymond Queneau

PIERROT MON AMI

Translated with a Preface by Barbara Wright

Introduction by Daniel Levin Becker

DALKEY ARCHIVE PRESS

Dallas / Rochester

Library of Congress Catalog Card Number: 87-72849
ISBN (pb): 978-1-628974-61-4 | ISBN (ebook): 978-1-62897-488-1

Interior design by Anuj Mathur
Cover design by Justin Childress

www.dalkeyarchive.com

Printed on permanent/durable acid-free paper and bound in the
United States of America.

Translator's Preface

A word about Queneau's style. It is strange. It is meant to be strange, and there is always an artistic reason for his deviations from the "usual."

All his life Queneau had a passionate love of language, of words. He considered that French writers had become so subservient to the strict rules of what was "correct," laid down over the centuries by the Academie Française, that their style had become fossilized. In comparison, he found the language of the man (and woman) in the street to be bubbling over with vitality, to be malleable, to be free. He decided: "I want to write in a living language—in the language of the ordinary man. The language you want to write in is your so-called maternal language." He determined to create "a *written* spoken language."

Naturally, Queneau was at first misunderstood, partly because his profound, deeply-considered philosophy is almost always overlaid with a mask of humor. If he's funny, he can't be serious, was the opinion of the upholders of long-outdated tradition. More thoughtful critics soon realized that he was in fact the innovator and liberator the French language had been needing for eons. And now, of course, he has become a classic—but a classic sui generis.

To me (and others), every book Queneau wrote forms a perfect, homogeneous whole. But within that homogeneous whole there is a plethora of the most heterogeneous elements, all of which, on analysis, are always in their right place and in the right proportion.

Inversion of the "usual" order of words in a phrase or sentence is one of these elements: its purpose is to lead gradually up to the most important word or notion it contains. And Queneau will amuse himself (and us) by contrasting within just a few lines the most down-to-earth colloquialisms with parodies of, for instance, the "noble" style. An example from *Pierrot*, taken at random: "Already laughs, already impatiences were vibrating." He will make people use expressions that at first seem totally out of character: Mounnezergues says that "it was June, the harsh, blood-red sun above the slates had only just risen over the roofs of Paris, a very thin mist was dancing over by the Bois de Boulogne. . . ." Would Mounnezergues talk like that? Well, why not? Don't we all have a would-be poetic side?

Other elements constantly used by Queneau are the sudden inclusion of technical terms, used strictly accurately ("found themselves obliged to slide on their dorsa"), unusual and intentionally pompous words ("salacity," "vibrionic")—but they exist, so why not use them if you feel like it? Especially when they fit in with two of the most important components of any text: the *tone* and the *rhythm*? Then, Queneau delights in an apparently chaotic change of tenses back and forth within the same sentence, but if you analyze them you will find that they accurately express a very slight nuance of time difference. Then there are intentional repetitions, as in the description of the fakir sticking great big hatpins into his cheeks: "Pierrot looked at this, pale with horror. Then the point reappeared between the two lips. Pierrot could hold out no longer. Pierrot fainted." Here, Queneau builds up a crescendo of phony horror—which ends in the bathos of a banal faint.

There are recondite allusions, anachronisms, neologisms (not many of the latter in *Pierrot*) of the word *ekcetera*. What what? you say to yourself. But when you listen carefully, not only in France, but in America, in England, and in other countries too, you may be surprised to discover that most of the time most people do in fact say *ek*cetera. Comic (as Queneau would say).

Queneau also likes, occasionally, to use the alienation effect, in order to remind us that what we are reading is a *fiction*. In his first novel, *Le Chiendent* (*The Bark Tree* / *Witch Grass*), one character says to another something like: "Are you a novelist?" and the other replies: "No, a character." There are similar examples here in *Pierrot*.

When asked in an interview with the writer and critic Georges Charbonnier how he decided on the mixture of elements in his books, Queneau replied that he thought the process was spontaneous and involuntary. One of the reasons for the quality and profundity of Queneau's writing is, I think, the way he combines his exceptionally conscious, analytic approach to his work with this simple trust in his unconscious feeling.

Queneau *enjoyed* the act of writing, and I think his enjoyment is contagious. One "should" never use the word "should" in considering his way of writing, but I will. Why "shouldn't" he amuse himself (and us, as I said before) if he wants to? Take the "mitocans" and "mocofans" who gawp at Mésange, who has moved behind the steering wheel of Pierrot's van, at the beginning of chapter 7. No French person has the slightest idea where these words come from, although it's clear what they mean. Queneau told me that they originated from his study of Romanian (a study he very soon abandoned), and that they are peasants of the most primitive kind. I recently had occasion to ask a Romanian writer about this. He laughed, and said: "Well, er, not exactly." They are in fact, it seems, a special kind of city slicker. Queneau would have been hugely delighted by this linguistic precision.

The question has to arise: Is all this translatable? One answer is that Queneau himself thought it was. When I secretly translated his *Exercises in Style* (which he had told me was the book of his that he would most like to see translated) (and the reason I did so in secret—it took me two years—was because I thought it couldn't be done), with a great deal of diffidence and no little terror I sent him the result. (He knew English well, having translated, among other books, Amos Tutuola's *The Palm-Wine Drinkard*.) He wrote immediately: "I have always thought that nothing is untranslatable. Here is new proof." And he added other compliments, which I will spare you. I just hope he would have thought the same about this translation of *Pierrot*, a novel in which, as Martin Esslin has said, "from the beginning the characters have a superabundance of wisdom," and which is surely one of Queneau's most beautiful books.

BARBARA WRIGHT

Introduction

I.

Uni Park, the fairground where we first meet Pierrot, and for that matter the majority of this novel's cast of characters, is modeled on a place that really existed in Neuilly-sur-Seine, a toney suburb just west of Paris. Luna Park, it was called, and Raymond Queneau frequented it for a time in his youth, recalling some years later its most arresting attraction: le Palais du Rire—remade by his light novelistic touch as le Palace de la Rigolade, and in turn by Barbara Wright as the Palace of Fun—a funhouse that culminated in the same spectacle we see Pierrot being trained to staff, in which "a draft of air lifted the skirts of the girls, held firmly in place by energetic employees." Visitors to the Palais du Rire could bypass this "absurd course," he notes, by paying five francs instead of one, which entitled them to a seat, near the exit, with an excellent view of the proceedings.

Queneau tells us this at the beginning of an essay called "Philosophes et voyous," a characteristically erudite and impious interrogation of the idea that a clean dialectical line can be drawn between the figure of the philosopher—melancholic, persecuted, probably bearded—and that of the . . . well, how to define *voyou*? He gives this some thought, surveying the literature, examining the word's etymology, going into surprisingly granular detail about Descartes's complexion, and quoting a nineteenth-century linguist who describes a *voyou* as one possessing all the vices of common people but none of their virtues. So: the pepper of the earth. Lowlife, hooligan, hoodlum, lout, rowdy, good-for-nothing, guttersnipe, ruffian, thug, scoundrel, punk. The word appears only twice in *Pierrot mon ami*, oddly enough, and Wright translates it once as "boys" and once as "toughs." On the other hand, you will note almost immediately, the novel has philosophers in spades—this being its term of art for the bawdy gawkers who come to see ladies' unmentionables and have a tendency to turn violent when they don't get the desired eyeful. (They're also called satyrs a few times: "that's the proper word," says Paradis.) True to life, at that: above the door at Luna Park through which the bearers of five-franc tickets were shown into the Palais de Rire, Queneau explains, read the legend *philosophers' entrance*.

All of this tracks. Queneau, a philosopher by education and temperament if not by vocation, was deeply and endur-ingly drawn to the *voyous* of the world, who people his fiction in generally unsensationalized form and who almost always have something of the sage about them. Not unlike the *néo-français* to which he dedicated so much energy throughout his remarkable publishing career—"the language of impropriety," as John Sturrock puts it, French as spoken by the demotic hordes rather than the stuffy gatekeepers—the intellectual legitimacy and spiritual value of the *voyou* in a world full of ostensibly loftier ideals was a concern that animated his work in both explicit and subterranean ways. In the middle of his disquisition on the philosopher–*voyou* distinction, he acknowledges the evidence that the latter more likely derives from *voie*, or thoroughfare—riffraff, street rat—than it does from *voir*, to see, from which we get *voyeur*—but reasons that *voyeur* isn't so far off either. For is the contemplation of female thighs and buttocks and undercarriages not, he asks, still a kind of contemplation?

II.

Pierrot mon ami was originally meant to be a detective novel. The *Don Quixote* of detective novels, even, per Queneau's preparatory notes. But over the course of its composition— and not for the first time in his bibliography—the characters developed their own opinions about their fate, and as their respective stories took shape through trial and error they manifested enough resistance that he finally capitulated and decided to make it a "simple picaresque" instead, with "no mystery" and "no police," but "adventures — yes / without solution." It would have "elements of chance and search," to which the reader would have direct access rather than being spoon-fed them by the travails of a detective. (This, the commentator Gilbert Pestureau concedes, is not ultimately true: the reader most certainly doesn't have *all* the elements, and that's assuming a logical explanation exists in the first place.) In press materials and interviews from the summer of 1942, Queneau doubled down, as in his response to a query from *Le Figaro* as to what he meant by "anti-detective novel":

> While writing *Pierrot mon ami*, I thought that the ideal detective novel (the reader having become too clever) would evidently be one where not only do we not know the criminal, but where we also don't even

know whether there's been a crime, and who the detective is. The idea may seem to you a bit abstract, perhaps . . . in any case, in *Pierrot mon ami*, there could be a detective novel, but there isn't one; we verge on a crime story, but don't fall into it; and naturally, in any event, the key is not given: the (clever) reader will find it by himself: "There is a certain pleasure in not knowing, because the imagination goes to work" (Claude Bernard).

And true enough, though it's far from necessary to your appreciation of the novel, it's instructive to imagine *Pierrot mon ami* as a detective story anyway, one that just happens to have been substantially hollowed of the genre's hallmarks and conventions, its intrigue and derring-do abandoned or obscured, leaving only what Mounnezergues calls "the shadow of an abstract idea floating over it, the shadow of an event." For in a sense we *do* have enough elements to cobble together some semblance of a mystery: the noisy and diverting setting, the cloudy motivations and vaguely conspiratorial complicities, the eccentricities and tasteful sprinkles of mysticism, the characters who may or may not be who they claim. We have carnies and savants and former soldiers, femmes fatales and honest matrons, a beleaguered entrepreneur, a fakir, a single-serving innkeeper who delivers a heartfelt soliloquy about the passing of time, two more or less well-behaved circus animals. We even have a former private detective turned *voyou* turned husband and father and "assistant torturer at the Palace of Fun," sent off late in the novel to "conduct an inquiry" that would do a great deal to illuminate its central mystery if only we could be sure what its central mystery *was*.

In short, we have the makings of a big rumbling romp of

an investigation, equal parts sinister and jubilant, entertaining and perplexing—it's just that the author took pains not to assemble them for us. Why be so restrictive? "How disappointing it is, the last chapter of a detective novel," Queneau continued in his response to *Le Figaro*, "with its strippings-bare and its exhibitions of dirty laundry." (The generative potential of a kit of spare parts from which the reader can construct their own detective novel is perhaps this book's most plausible connection to the Oulipo, the experimentalist literary workshop Queneau would co-found eighteen years later with François Le Lionnais, a polymath who once inventoried the possible endings to murder mysteries and concluded that the only thing that hadn't been tried yet was the culprit turning out to be the reader.) He'd rather let us let our imaginations go to work as we read, as we watch and observe and wonder, as we wait for an eyeful of something titillatingly both hidden and not.

And in this we have no better avatar, no better titular friend, than Pierrot: the "interested onlooker," the world-weary tumbleweed who has "no particular opinion on public morals, or the future of civilization," the near-sighted observer who without his glasses—Wright calls them *cheaters*—can't see more than five meters in front of him. Pierrot is an ingenious stand-in for both detective and reader in Queneau's universe, and his consistent impassiveness throughout the book is one of its most extraordinary features: he's lost and unbothered about it, adrift and routinely bored—who in a mystery is ever *bored?*—not incurious or desireless, exactly, but above all content to let the novel happen around him, *to* him, his actions and interactions rippling out in an ever-stranger butterfly effect. He examines it all "with the severity of the connoisseur untrammeled by all the worries of possession, but with the satisfaction afforded by this disinterestedness." We might call him an antihero, not in the modern prestige-drama sense of the word but in homage to his role at the front—or the rear, it's hard to tell—of a novel that is already so willfully *anti*.

III.

About that "light novelistic touch."

Queneau wrote quickly and with evident relish. Alongside his poems and essays and journals and translations, alongside his work as an editor at the big-deal French publishing house Gallimard and his personal readings that could easily have occupied a full-time schedule for a normal person, he seemed to always have a novel in progress; writ large, his fictional output reads like a sort of intellectual ticker tape, pinched off every so often (indeed, impressively often: *Pierrot mon ami* took him all of six months) into a sparkling filmstrip of invention and exploration, steeped in the vapors of whatever was passing through his head. We read his ideas and opinions, his infatuations and eyerolls, his ambient and abiding fascinations: detective stories, yes; philosophy, yes, and its earthly obverse; linguistics, cinema, mathematics, madness—it would be easier to enumerate the things that didn't interest Queneau, in which he didn't have some weirdly total field of mastery. But a primary staple among those fascinations, one always present in greater or lesser quantity across four decades of ticker tape, was the construct of the novel itself.

In 1937 he published a short essay called "Technique of the Novel," in which he memorably grouses that anyone can push a handful of more or less lifelike characters across a field like a flock of geese and call the result a novel. He proceeds to lay out some of the numerological mechanisms at work in three of his own novels, arguing not dogmatically but by demonstration—this is the same anti-doctrinaire spirit he instilled in the Oulipo—for an alternative that replaces that narrative laxity with rigor and deliberation, an attention to form that's conscious and concrete even if it doesn't necessarily appear as such to the reader. He would bear out this quietly seditious idea in endlessly bewitching ways from his first novel, 1933's *The Bark Tree* (later reissued as *Witch Grass*), whose protagonist begins as a silhouette, to his last, 1967's gleefully fourth wall–demolishing *The Flight of Icarus*, in which a protagonist goes missing from a manuscript and strikes out on his own. (Sound familiar?) But if Queneau also wrote poems that poked fun at poetry and poets, also curated curiosities that trick a simple story into serving as a *reductio ad absurdum* of storytelling—these include *Exercises in Style*, which recounts the same mundane anecdote in ninety-nine different forms and registers, and "Un conte à votre façon," probably the first choose-your-own-adventure narrative in history—his novelistic self-interrogations have a somewhat more existential cast. Without ever quite succumbing to despondency or nihilism or schmaltz, they nonetheless wrestle with the question of what business the novel has pretending to be more than a shallow entertainment, aspiring to speak mimetically to real life, "imposing a post hoc determinism on a sequence of events whose unpredictability," as Sturrock writes, "was its prime attraction when we set out." Such artifice, rewarding as it can be to read, gratifying as it can be to create, is a presumption the novelist comes by no more legitimately than the god Queneau was too skeptical, too mathematically minded, to believe in.

IV.

The particular way this ambivalence manifests in *Pierrot*—aside from the deadpan humor, lexico-tonal oddities, and fractious playfulness that come standard in any Queneau production—is a spirit of demurral suspended somewhere between Pierrot's own stalwart indifference and the politely obstinate refusal of Melville's Bartleby. That is, what inevitably meets the casual eye and the oulipian loupe alike is how actively this novel persists in repudiating or undermining, or at the very least complicating—we can't say Queneau ditched the *Don Quixote* ambition altogether—its own status as a novel, detective or otherwise. It seems to always be fraying the ropes that hold its set pieces in place, missing its lighting cues, losing track of which of its characters are primary and which silhouettes. They're a good flock of geese, these characters: they go about their lives, have their little passions and adventures or covet those of others, abide by their values and preoccupations with "perfect although inexplicable fidelity." But sometimes they arrive too late to the action, sometimes they're nowhere in its vicinity, sometimes the events that seem most decisive turn out to mean nothing, or probably nothing. Like the mystery plot, the gears and cogs are there if you look for them, but what you see when you stand back is how much care and consideration have gone into building a story that appears to answer to no identifiable logic.

But then logic need not be identifiable to exist—this may be the cheeriest Quenellian theology it's possible to articulate—and perhaps even the repudiations have their own intelligent design. Whether the stories that originate in the fairground and sprawl forth into the surrounding world are held and manipulated "at the extremities of a taut, extensile wire" or whether they're genuinely disjointed and random, a true adventure without solution, what does it matter? For Queneau, asking the question is enough. Good thing, because no answer is forthcoming. "No doubt about it," Pierrot remarks to himself after yet another coincidental encounter with a silhouette who used to hang around Uni Park, "someone has deliberately strewn this route with people who used to live in that district." In his perfectly self-possessed fashion, though, rather than investigate or prolong the story, his own or anyone else's, Pierrot prefers to go to the movies.

Do *Pierrot*'s characters know they're in a novel? Do they suspect as much? Could it be that that's the shadow of a mystery they're trying, never quite consciously, to unravel? It's a fetching thought, though of course it's not that simple. In the book's epilogue, instead of the dismal all-is-revealed last chapter, Queneau delivers a stunning summation where, a year after the week in which most of the novel's events are clustered—"the most autonomous episode of his life"—Pierrot looks back and sees both "the novel it could have made" and "the novel it *had* become, a novel so shorn of artifice that it was quite impossible to know whether it contained a riddle to be solved or whether it did not." In this moment of hindsight, this premature past tense, it's as if the myopic Pierrot—and for that matter the myopic Queneau—is absolved of his presence and participation in something as banal as this humble entertainment. Then he continues on his way and encounters a few of his fellow characters, ones with whom his path was briefly but meaningfully intertwined. Only one of them remembers who he is.

And what about us, the too-clever readers—do we know we're reading a novel? Are we meant to identify with our friend Pierrot, the bemused bespectacled observer? Or with Yvonne, absently indulging the various would-be charmers who cross her path? Or with Mounnezergues, ever attentive to the shadow of mystery hanging over the place, or with Pradonet, haunted by the incompletion of the edifice he once meant to create, or with Léonie, convinced an answer is out there, patiently waiting to be tracked down? Are we philosophers, shelling out to contemplate characters in compromising positions, or are we *voyous*, peering over the shoulder of a stranger on the bus, skimming recklessly over these strange pristine sentences, taking from the text only what serves us? By refusing to decide for us, Queneau gives us the gift of being all of them at once, validating whatever we want the novel, this novel, to be. All we have to do is look.

Daniel Levin Becker
Paris, September 2022

1

"Take your specs off then," said Tortose to Pierrot, "take your specs off then if you want to look the part."

Pierrot obeyed and put them carefully away in their case. He could still see about five meters in front of him, but the barrel and the spectators' seats were shrouded in fog.

"Well then you see," Tortose—Monsieur Tortose—went on, "you grab them when they get up to the cakewalk, you grab them by the wrists, you hold 'em tight, and then you plunk them down over the blowhole. How long you leave them there, that's a matter of tact, there's special cases, you just have to learn. Right. We'll have a tryout, I'll be the woman, there you go, I come in from here, when I get to the cakewalk I naturally hesitate, you grab me by the wrists, that's it, and then you lug me along, that's right, and you plunk me down over the blowhole, very good. Got it?"

"Got it, Monsieur Tortose."

"Go down out now then with Petit-Pouce and Paradis and wait for the suckers. Understood?"

"Understood, Monsieur Tortose."

Pierrot put his glasses on again and went to join Petit-Pouce and Paradis, who were smoking in silence. It was still light, but already crepuscularly so; the thermometer registered a nice little average temperature which made you want to enjoy the fine weather without talking. People were mooching around in the alleyways but the crowd wasn't compact enough to be much fun. Only the bumper cars were beginning to ram each other on Perdrix's Dodgem Track. The other rides were still deserted, but their organs were booming and their nostalgic music certainly contributed to the evolution of the inner life of the employees of the Palace of Fun. At her cash desk, Madame Tortose was knitting.

Couples and groups and, more rarely, individuals, passed up and down, still in a state of dissemination, still not agglomerated into crowds, laughing in moderation. Petit-Pouce, who had finished his cigarette, stubbed its embers against his heel and with his thumb and forefinger ejected the butt to an appreciable distance.

"Well, chummy," he said to Pierrot, "d'you think you're going to like grafting with us?"

"It's not too tiring for the moment."

"Yes, but you just wait until midnight."

Paradis, turning to Pierrot, said to Petit-Pouce:

"He's the one that clocked up sixty-seven thousand on a Coney Island."

Of all the one-franc pinball games, Coney Island requires the most skill. You have to score twenty thousand to be entitled to a free game, and those who achieve this are rare. Pierrot, though, generally scored forty thousand, and once, even, in Paradis's presence, sixty-seven thousand, which had been the origin of their relationship.

"It has happened," said Pierrot modestly.

"We'll have a go together," said Petit-Pouce, "because I sometimes give it a whirl too."

"Oh, you're no match for him," said Paradis, who had a high opinion of Pierrot without, however, extending his admiration beyond the domain of one-franc pinball games at which, it is true, Pierrot excelled. And in any case, as this friendship was only a week old, he hadn't yet either had the time or taken the trouble to interest himself in the other aspects of the personality of his new pal.

There was now a solitary customer in the Squirrel's Treadmill, putting his all into describing the circumference of his cage at three francs for a quarter-of-an-hour. The Alpinic Railway was practicing rumbling with its still-empty cars. But the merry-go-rounds were still not revolving, the Palais de Danse was deserted, and the clairvoyants weren't seeing anything coming.

"There's not a lot of people yet," said Pierrot, trying to find a neutral subject, because he didn't want Paradis's eulogies to get him, Pierrot, in bad with him, Petit-Pouce, so that the sight of him, Pierrot, finally made him, Petit-Pouce, sick, but sick! In any case, Pierrot, who had had a hard childhood, a painful adolescence and a difficult youth (which was not yet over), and who therefore knew the way of the world, Pierrot was now sure of one thing: sooner or later sparks would certainly fly between him and Petit-Pouce, unless it was with Paradis, who can tell?

"We'll have a go," Petit-Pouce repeated; he didn't allow himself to be sidetracked, because he liked competition.

He would have carried on arguing the toss in this direction (that of one-franc pinball games) had not two little skirts, arm in arm and on the lookout for gallants, passed by under his nose.

"The one on the right's a good-looker," he said authoritatively. "A nice bit of stuff."

"Well now, Ladies," Paradis shouted, "aren't you going to treat yourselves to a bit of fun?"

"Walk in, Ladies," Petit-Pouce yelled, "walk in!"

They did an about-turn and passed the Palace again, as near to it as they could get.

"Well now, Ladies," said Petit-Pouce, "don't you like the look of our joint? Ah! the fun that goes on there."

"Oh, I know," said one.

"And anyway, there's not a cat there," said the other.

"That's just it," cried Paradis, "we were just waiting for yours."

"Haven't done yourself an injury, have you?" they asked, "because to think that one up all by yourself, have to make an effort, and that can be dangerous."

"Ha ha, they're one up on you," said Petit-Pouce.

They began to laugh, all five of them, every last one of them. Seeing and hearing this, some of the passersby began to take an interest in the Palace of Fun. Madame Tortose, sensing that the harvest was ready to be reaped, put down her knitting and got out the tickets. With the two little skirts as bait, the philosophers would soon be turning up, that was for sure, and the poor fish would go hog-wild to get a seat that would give them a good view of the rest. A line formed, consisting of those errand boys, clerks and school kids prepared to lay out twenty sous to see a bit of thigh.

"How about a go for free?" Petit-Pouce suggested.

That would warm up the audience, that'd encourage the philosophers, and once it had got going, the evening would simply have to carry on from performance to performance until round about midnight, with some nice takings at the end of the day for Signor Tortose, and sweat-drenched shirts for the three athletes. But the two kids, no fools, considered that a go for free would be a gift—on their part.

"Thanks a lot," said one, "you'd have to pay us to get us into a thing like that."

"Roll up, roll up, the show's starting!" Petit-Pouce yelled at the rubbernecks.

"And you, get to work," said Paradis to Pierrot, who hastened to obey.

And they ditched the chicks.

Everything in Uni Park was now rumbling and roaring, and the crowd, both male and female, was spreading out in thick tentacles in the direction of the attractions on offer, sometimes at a high price, relatively speaking that is: two or three francs, in general. Opposite the Palace of Fun, aeroplanes were gliding, attached to a tall tower by steel wires, and in front of the Palace itself, great was the animation. People were buying their tickets, following Petit-Pouce's injunctions. Those who wanted to be subjected to the mechanical shenanigans paid twenty sous, whereas the philosophers shelled out three times that sum, impatient as they were at feeling themselves all ready for an eyeful. Pierrot went back to his place, put his cheaters away, and waited. Already laughs, already impatiences were vibrating.

The first customers of both sexes appeared at the top of a moving staircase, dazzled by a spotlight, aghast at finding themselves thus exposed without warning, the men to the malignancy of the audience, the women to its salacity. Disembarked from their staircase by the force of circumstance, they consequently found themselves obliged to slide on their dorsa down an assiduously-polished slope. The philosophers were already able to utilize their visual capacities to the maximum of their output, each one demanding from the functioning of this sense, clarity, rapidity, perspicacity, photographicity. But this was still nothing, not even as much as the low flight of swallows is a presage of rain. It must indeed be understood that such a spectacle, reduced to the minimum, may occur in the course of the most banal everyday life, a fall in the metro, a slip on getting out of a bus, a tumble on a too well-polished floor. In this, there was still practically nothing of the emotive specificity that the philosophers had come to find for the price of three francs in the Palace of Fun.

Meanwhile, maliciously-calculated indignities pursued the buffs' every step: staircases whose steps collapsed horizontally, planks that jumped up at a right angle or curved in and became a basin, a conveyor belt that moved in alternate directions, floors that consisted of strips shaken with a Brownian movement. And more. Pierrot's job was to get the people out of this impasse. With the men, it was enough to give them a hand, but when a woman, terrified by this difficult passage, came along, you grabbed her by the wrists, you lugged her, you tugged her, and you finally plunked her down over an air vent that sent her skirts billowing up—the first treat for the philosophers, if this flurry revealed enough thigh. This rapid prelude was completed by the exit from the barrel, after a vague labyrinth imposed on the patients. And anyway, the first glimpse already prepares the apotheosis; in convulsive expectation, the philosophers spot the choice morsels and squint at them with dilated eyes and blazing pupils.

After the labyrinth, then, the victims were faced with a cylinder revolving around its axis into which they had to venture in order to come to the end of all the pleasures they had bought with their twenty sous. Some came out of it with honor: totally uninteresting. Others lost their balance and collapsed, got sucked into the rotation and writhed, rolled over, squirmed, rolled back, corkscrewed, to the greatest diversion of those who, already released from the ordeal, had joined the group of philosophers. As for the latter, they weren't so specially amused by these pirouettes and whirligigs. They were less interested in the ridiculousness of the louts than in the deshabille of the females, one of whom had just appeared at the entrance to the barrel and was jibbing at the undertaking, for fear of falling. So Petit-Pouce grabbed her by the arms and, half-carrying her, got her through the contraption without mishap; once outside it, however, he put her down over an air vent which blew up her dress and revealed two legs and some frillies: the delighted philosophers applauded, while some persons of an innocent turn of mind were content to laugh at the misadventure that had happened to the lady. One, following on behind, seeing the said misadventure and wishing to avoid it, refused to follow Petit-Pouce, who had gone back in search of victims, but he grabbed her. The audience roared approval. He pulled her along, a silence fell in expectation of the supreme indiscretion, and he deposited her on the allotted spot and held her there longer than the other one, to secure the vengeance of the philosophers, who had been excited by the attempted refusal. A third was ardently awaited by the satyrs because the first blowhole had given them cause to hope for underwear reduced to the minimum.

"Don't miss her," an enthusiast shouted to Petit-Pouce, while Paradis was moving people along to allow the first row to have an unobstructed view.

Petit-Pouce made it with her: a triumph. It wasn't quite clear whether the lady was outraged or whether she had come there to display her charms. There were three or four more, but they were much less interesting, and then it was the end of the first show. The vulgar shoved off, but the fanatics remained. Paradis went round to collect the money. Petit-Pouce acquired a few gratuities intended to incite him to take special care of the prettiest girls. Pierrot wiped his forehead, because this was real work, all the more so in that the fleshly charms of some of the birds added up to quite a weight; and all this gave him, Pierrot, no pleasure at all, as on the one hand he was too busy with his transport duties, and on the other the restriction of the field of action of his range of vision prevented him from enjoying to the full the beauties revealed at the exit from the barrel.

Meanwhile Petit-Pouce and Paradis, yelling outside the door, had rounded up a new group of fun-lovers, and a new show began. The philosophers (those who also had a passion for crossword puzzles) folded their newspapers, started to fidget on their seats, and peacefully prepared themselves to get an eyeful. And once again Pierrot and Petit-Pouce, the one here and the other there, roughly grabbed hold of ladies who fought and wriggled, humiliated and applauded. Pierrot was beginning to get his hand in and to practice his new profession mechanically. Come on, then, the little blonde, and he thought about his father, he was dead, a decent sort, who took a drop too much but was merry in his cups, and who materialized with the soup, whose steam seemed to condense into a human aspect. Come on, you, the big brunette, and he thought about his mother, also dead, who had dealt him so many wallops that he could still feel the bruises, he believed. One more little blonde, one more brunette, and then here comes an old one, and now it's a little girl, and he went on thinking about those far-off days of which only scraps remained; it may perhaps have been by chance that he was thinking of them this evening, perhaps also because of his new job which was ushering in, who knows? a new life, and in shaking up these tatters he gave rise to whole flights of pale, quivering butterflies.

Come on, then, the big brunette, move up and let me get hold of you, and he was thinking that it isn't funny to have had a childhood like his, it goes sour on you, it goes mouldy, and the good bits where you can look back and see you were so nice and so full of hope are forever tarnished by the rest.

"Hey you, the flunky, hands off, eh."

Pierrot let the last clothes moths take wing and then caught sight of an intimidating individual who was indubitably a pimp. Despite the imminent danger, his professional conscience didn't flinch. He tried to get hold of the damsel in spite of her ponce's veto. She resisted. The crowd began to snarl. Pierrot insisted, labored, conquered: the chippie had to follow him.

The applause was great. But the disappointment was about to be equally great. The mack, who had followed close on his woman's heels, held her skirt down with both hands, which annihilated the effect of the blowhole.

An indignant, unanimous, deafening clamor arose.

"Cuckold!" a philosopher yelled.

"Cuckold! Cuckold!" the audience echoed.

"If we can't even enjoy ourselves any more," said a very respectable gentleman.

Behind the moralist and his paramour was another couple of the same nature. The second he's-my-man naturally imitated his buddy. Twice frustrated of their pleasure, the philosophers began to swarm, but the two villains carried on regardless, defying their adversaries, and with every rejoinder the abuse hurled from one group to another increased in both vigor and obscenity. The principal physiological functions of the human body were invoked by the ones as by the others, as also were the different organs situated between the knee and the waist. Actions lent renewed force to words undermined by too-frequent usage. When the quadrille reached the barrel, there was great excitement. The two macks didn't wish to deliver their pavement princesses into Paradis's hands. The gentlemen had an animated discussion while the cylinder revolved without a load and the expectant onlookers howled their scorn for a prudery that was out of place in these surroundings, especially when it came from such suspicious characters.

"Bastards! Bastards!" they declared.

Paradis finally realized that he must follow the boss's advice: no trouble. He pressed a lever, the rotation stopped, and the two bozos, followed by their ladies, strolled through triumphant and mocking. One of the philosophers couldn't take this insult. Exasperated at seeing himself robbed of the particular pleasure for which he had paid three francs, he left his seat, jumped up on to the platform and joined battle. His fist reverberated on the eye of one of the individuals, but the latter's buddy countered unhesitatingly and destroyed one of the aggressor's ears with a punch that was no less apposite than expert. Whereupon the philosopher, his eyes bulging with pain, made a headlong, gundog rush on his adversaries and all three went rolling over on the ground. Paradis and Petit-Pouce tried to separate them but some other philosophers, inspired by this example, darted into the fray, shoved the two employees aside and started walking enthusiastically over the entwined wrestlers. Thereupon a few louche individuals, their instincts aroused and their sympathies engaged, decided to take up their colleagues' cause, and fell upon the philosophers tooth and nail and fist. An officer of the law who tried to intervene was cast out of the vortex by the centrifugal virtue of the combatants' ardor. Paradis was mopping his nose, Petit-Pouce was rubbing his ribs, the crowd was on its feet, bawling with joy and indignation.

Pierrot had remained in his place, from which he caught a glimpse of the dusty mêlée through a fog and, as no one was taking an interest in his activities any longer, he put his glasses back on. Having examined the situation, he did not for an instant doubt that his presence was necessary and, jumping over the railings, he plunged into the heap. First his cheaters were ejected, and then himself, with a rapidly blackening eye. He retrieved his glasses, only one of which was cracked, and sat down in a corner. He had done as much as his mates.

They were now watching the barney with interest, but disinterestedness. And if a broken tooth or a bit of nose bitten off and then spat out happened to roll in their direction, they were content to brush it aside with the back of their hand, and then wipe off the blood that had sullied it.

But Monsieur Tortose, who has been alerted, calls the police, and soon their white batons are resounding on the frantic skulls. The prestige of the constables, their prestige above all, dissipates the confusion as the point of a sword disintegrates a ghost, and the energetically-emptied theater of operations now exhibited no more than the tattered velvet of its seats and the trampled dust of its floor.

The guv'nor of the Palace of Fun, advised by the competent authorities that his attraction would be closed down for the rest of the evening, entered, examined velvet and dust, slides and barrel, sniffed, and slowly approached his three employees who were rubbing and brushing themselves, trying to make themselves look respectable.

"Lot of bastards," he murmured. "Lot of bastards," he declared in a hollow voice. "Lot of bastards," he yelled.

Silent, they examined him.

"Lot of bastards," he yelled once again.

"Ah, guv, if you'd only seen it," said Paradis with fervor. "The big bloke comes up. You're looking for trouble, he tells me. Biff bang, right away, my fist in both his eyes, then wallop, my left in the pit of his stomach, in short, fatty's down, without another word."

"Okay, okay," said Monsieur Tortose. "I'm not that gullible. You behaved like slobs, yellow bellies, imbeciles. Not even capable of dealing with a simple matter like that! Go on, out, beat it!"

"Oh no, guv," said Paradis, "have a heart. We don't get jokers like that every day. We've done the job properly so far. The philosophers were happy. Things were going fine."

"I'm not saying," said Monsieur Tortose.

"I even heard the philosophers," Paradis went on, "I even heard them saying to each other: those young fellows, they know how to handle the bints, when they're on we don't miss a mouthful, it isn't money down the drain, we get a lot of pleasure for it. That's what they were saying to each other, and they went on: me, I'll be back every evening."

"Yep, that's true," said Petit-Pouce, "I heard them: exactly those words."

"You can see they aren't bad lads," said Madame Tortose, who had just cashed up and joined her spouse. "You aren't going to make them lose their season's work on account of a dirty rat like that. It wasn't their fault"

"Oh! thank you very much, Madame," said Paradis.

"Right, that'll do," said Monsieur Tortose. "That'll do. Come back tomorrow."

"Shall we lock up?" asked Petit-Pouce.

"Yes. And then you can go home to bed, if you feel like it."

"Right, guv. We'll shut up shop and go for a walk."

They shut up shop and went for a walk.

They went to the nearest point, that's to say they didn't leave Uni Park, on which this June Sunday was bestowing both fine weather and crowds in abundance, the conjugation of which produced a black, bawling ebullience inundated by the lights and music of more than twenty attractions. On this one you go round in circles and on that one you fall from a great height, on this one you travel at speed and on that one all askew, here you get jostled and there you get bumped, everywhere you get your innards churned up and you laugh, you grope a bit of prat and you feel a bit of tit, you try your skill and you measure your strength, and you laugh, you let yourself go, you eat dust.

Pierrot, Petit-Pouce and Paradis leant over the balustrade

round the bumper car track and examined the situation. As usual, it contained couples (of no interest), men on their own, women on their own. The whole object was for the men on their own to ram the women on their own. A few men on their own who were very young, still in all the flower of their naïvety, are content with the joys of vanity and apply themselves to the task of describing ellipses without bumping into anything. Perhaps this is their way of consoling themselves for not having a real car. As for the women on their own, naturally there can be two of them in the same car, this doesn't stop them being on their own, with the exception of extreme, more or less Sapphic, cases.

Petit-Pouce and Paradis, having shaken the mitts of a few colleagues whose task consisted in flitting from car to car to get the buffs to pay up (some of them stayed put the whole evening), Petit-Pouce and Paradis spotted one of these same bi-female couples and recognized the two little skirts who had started the evening outside the Palace. They waited patiently until from impact to impact the girls passed close by them and then, quite shamelessly, began to holler at them. At first the girls turned up their noses at these advances and continued their peregrinations, but when a general mêlée had penned them in facing their gallants, they finally deigned to smile.

When the bell rang to signal the renewal of the disbursements, Petit-Pouce and Paradis climbed over the railing and threw themselves into a vehicle. As soon as the bell announced the resumption of hostilities, they set out in pursuit of the two children with a view to percussing them. And hoopla! Having thus become amply acquainted, at the next bell a chassé-croisé divided these four persons into two heterosexual couples. Petit-Pouce chose the curly-haired brunette and Paradis took the peroxide blonde. Pierrot neither chose nor took anything.

Leaning comfortably on his elbows, Pierrot was thinking about the death of Louis XVI, which means, specifically, about nothing in particular; his mind contained nothing but a mental, light, and almost luminous mist, like the fog on a beautiful winter morning, nothing but a flight of anonymous midges. The cars were energetically ramming each other, the trolley wires crepitating against the metal net, women were screaming, and, farther off, all over the rest of Uni Park, there was the hubbub of the crowds enjoying themselves, the clamor of the charlatans and clowns doing their tricks, and the rumble of the machines wearing themselves out. Pierrot had no particular opinion on public morals, or the future of civilization. No one had ever told him that he was intelligent. He had frequently been told, rather, that he behaved like an idiot or that he bore some resemblance to the moon. At all events, here and now, he was happy, and content, vaguely. Besides, among the midges there was one that was bigger than the others, and more insistent. Pierrot had a job, at least for the season. In October, he'd see. For the moment, he had a third of a year ahead of him and it was already chinking with the simoleons of his pay. That was something to be happy and content about for someone who had a permanent knowledge of uncertain days, unlikely weeks, and very deficient months. His black eye hurt a little, but has physical suffering ever precluded happiness?

For Petit-Pouce and Paradis, for them, life was beautiful, really it was. With one arm round the tail of a succulent quail, with the other nonchalantly manipulating the steering wheel of their vehicle, they were treating themselves to happiness at forty sous for five minutes. They were getting twofold enjoyment out of their sense of touch; directly, from the contact of a rib or a breast through a minimum layer of material, and indirectly from the bumps they imposed or more rarely sustained. Their vanity also was getting twofold enjoyment, directly from

bumping far more frequently than they were bumped, and
indirectly from thinking of Pierrot whom they had left standing, and on his own. And with the music as a bonus, a loud-
speaker bellowing "Oh my love. I'm yours forever," there was
really enough to allow the tingles of the dolce vita to run up
and down your spine, which only goes to show that it has been
proved that you can very well not think about the death of
Louis XVI and still go on existing with at least an appearance
of humanity and with pleasure in your heart.

Meanwhile, during the entr'actes, Petit-Pouce was not such
a happy man as all that. Because he was married, very legitimately. And he had qualms. Only little tiny ones, but qualms
just the same. Hence, while pulling his deuce out of his pocket,
he merely applied more pressure on the young breast on which
his fingers were planted.

Seeing that his mates were about to have another go,
Pierrot turned away; he'd had enough. Opposite him was the
Babylonian mass of the Alpinic Railway with the occasional
string of cars hurtling down carrying some female hysterias
with it. On his right the philosophers, dispersed by the police,
had regrouped, nose in air, and were watching the determined
efforts of a strapping young man sweating his guts out in the
nearby Squirrel's Treadmill. On his left was a succession of
shooting galleries, games and tombolas. He went down that
way. He had a vague desire to try his skill at demolishing a pyr-
amid of five empty cans with four balls, or at photographing
himself with a rifle shot. He strolled on, carried along by the
crowd, sometimes stationary like an abandoned wreck washed
up on the shore, then strolling again, as if caught up anew in
the maelstrom of a triumphant charge by the waves. He wasn't
tempted by The Compleat Angler, Grannie's Crocks, or The
Sleeping Beauty, but The Machine Gun Range attracted him.

Oddly enough, the manipulation of this weapon didn't

seem to be tempting anyone. The contraption did indeed look fearsome. Pierrot went up to it.

He handed over his forty sous and filled a target. It wasn't very good.

"Not up to much," he said to the girl in charge of the stand.

He tried again. It was still mediocre.

"It doesn't surprise me. With my eye."

"Have you been in a fight?"

"Nothing special. At the Palace of Fun, just now."

"Ah yes, I've already heard about it. What happened?"

He told her.

"Isn't that idiotic?" she concluded.

"You haven't got many customers," Pierrot remarked. He could make allusions to the trade, now he'd shown he belonged.

"I'm in a bad place. People stop at Grannie's Crocks and then cross over to The Sleeping Beauty, leaving me out. It's the idiotic amusements that attract them. With you, at least, it's the sport."

Pierrot looked at her.

"Me, I'd come just for you."

"My my."

"I mean it. And anyway, I'm sure there's loads of guys that come to chat you up, pretending to amuse themselves with this gadget."

"Yes, that's true. There's some that's like leeches . . . No way to get rid of them. And stupid into the bargain . . . So stupid . . ."

"Well yes, some of them are wood from the neck up."

"They think they're smart, but they talk nothing but eye-wash, utter rubbish . . . And their jokes—as obvious as they are."

"I can see it from here," said Pierrot.

"You, you don't seem to be like them."

"Mustn't compliment me on that," said Pierrot. "I don't do it on purpose."

"Yes, you aren't like them. For instance, you haven't asked me for a date yet."

"Shall I wait for you at the exit?" Pierrot asked.

"The thing is, I'm a young lady," said the bint. "I have a papa who keeps his eye on me. I also have a stepmother, not a real one, one my father married without benefit of clergy or even of Monsieur le Maire, but who's just as much of a piece of crap as if she was a real one. What about you?"

"I'm just a poor orphan," said Pierrot.

"Any brothers or sisters?"

"No."

"You must be lonely."

"Oh no, I haven't got that sort of temperament. It gets me sometimes, but only just like everyone else."

"Me neither, I'm not the sort of person to let myself wither away."

"And what would you say to our meeting again one of these days? Tomorrow?"

Swinging his head halfway round to the right, Pierrot took a squint behind him.

"Are you looking at that hustler?" he was asked.

"Me? Oh no. I was looking to see what had become of my pals. They're on the dodgems, over there."

"Will you treat me to a ride?"

"Yes. But when?"

"Right now. I'll put this thing away."

She muffled the machine gun up in a black oilcloth cover, put the ammunition away in a padlocked box, and tipped the takings into her handbag.

"There we are," she said, "let's go."

Three ponces appeared, who looked like real plug-uglies.

"Not so fast. Mam'zelle," said the most thuglike one, "kindly unwrap this contraption and let us have a few bangs."

The other two considered this a marvelous crack. They burst out laughing like a hundred farts.

"Have to come again," said Pierrot's possible girlfriend. "We're closing."

"What d'you mean closing? At this hour?"

"That's the way it is."

The men hesitated. Pierrot took off his glasses. She said to him:

"Take no notice. They're just wankers."

They stood there like dummies. The most big-mouthed one, the orator, looked at Pierrot's black eye uncertainly. Proof of aggressive courage? or of easy defeat? However, he didn't have to reflect for very long, for, brushed aside by his lady interlocutor with a sure and, upon my word, vigorous gesture, he could do nothing but gawp, on the one hand, at the backs of two people walking away from him with scorn and dignity, and on the other at a weapon tied up in its enveloping oilcloth. So he departed with his two companions, quite sad.

Pierrot was not displeased at having avoided a new schemozzle, not that he was a coward, but well, it didn't amuse him. The girl had taken his arm. She was all warm by his side, and elastic. She wore perfume, painted her nails and rouged her lips. Pierrot felt, inhaled, admired all this. He thought it was terrific. She was almost as tall as he, blonde, or more or less, with the rather delicate face of a tuberculous film star, and as regards the rest, well built. Pierrot put his gig-lamps back on and invited her to a ride on the bumper cars.

They inserted themselves into one of these little vehicles,

and they were off. Pierrot shot forward. The first car he caromed off also contained a couple similarly squeezed. The man, who considered himself skillful, turned round to make a mental note of the brazen fellow who had shown him such scant respect. This man was called Petit-Pouce. He was short, stocky, solidly built, forty-five years old, married but still playing the field, a native of Bezons, an elector in the eleventh arrondissement, getting pretty thin on top, in short, a hothead. And then, if anyone was astonished it was he, Petit-Pouce, when he caught sight of Pierrot with a doll by his side. In his amazement, he allowed himself to be rammed by Paradis who, seeing the same sight, lost control of his plaything, which led to a really very satisfactory general pileup.

Meanwhile Pierrot had resumed his course, and was elegantly describing lemniscates and conchoids. And the beautiful child was snuggling up to him. They were very contented, both of them, in the midst of a considerable noise. Of the various fragrances that came crowding into his nostrils, rubber, metal, varnish, dust, and others, the only one Pierrot retained was the voluptuous Houbigant with which the little pretty had impregnated herself. The scents caused him some emotion, and immersed him in a luminous, spangled fog.

It was through this haze of perfumed stars that he gradually began to distinguish two personages who seemed to be taking an interest in him. One was a still-young woman, a platinum blonde, pompously made up, tall and stout. The other was a man of similar age and of equally considerable dimensions. The woman was pointing her finger at him, at him, Pierrot. Pierrot wondered for a moment if it really was he who was being denounced with such vehemence. But there's no doubt about it. It really is he. And yet he doesn't know this lady. She seems to be triumphing, sneering, threatening. In short, all kinds of emotions are chasing around on her face. The fog has dispersed. Pierrot can see her very clearly now. As for the bloke, he has a funny sort of mug. The top is fairly well laid out, but after the halfway point of the nose, everything does a vanishing act. The cheeks have sunk into the bottom of the jaws, unevenly. One nostril opens wider than the other. As for the ears, they flap in the wind.

The bell rang, and the cars stopped. Pierrot was just going to suggest another go when he realized that the blonde virago's denunciations were going to cause trouble. And indeed, the fellow with her stepped over the balustrade and headed for him.

"What the hell are you doing there?" he yelled. "What about the machine gun? Eh? What about the machine gun?"

Observing that this discourse was addressed to his potential girlfriend, Pierrot turned round to her; she had already disappeared. Meanwhile, the crowd was splitting its sides, so delectable did it consider this adventure. As for Paradis and Petit-Pouce, they were crying with laughter at this colossal drollery.

The girl having fled, the infuriated fellow turned his wrath on the bespectacled seducer, who was extricating himself from his car.

"You," said he, "*you* can get the hell out of here. Just because you paid three francs at the gate, that doesn't mean you've bought the right to debauch the personnel. Does it?"

"No, of course not," Pierrot conceded. "Only, I didn't pay three francs."

He didn't wish to let this little error pass.

"Did you get in half price?" the fellow asked. "But you're not a soldier."

"No," Pierrot once again conceded. "I got in for free."

"Well, that's the end," bawled the stentor.

He made gestures to invite the spectators to savor this derision.

"You wouldn't be making fun of me by any chance?" he asked.

Pierrot would very much have liked to know who he was, this big, muscular fellow.

"I simply wanted to tell you that I work here."

"You? You work here? And since when?"

"Since today."

Was not this the honest truth? And yet the inquisitor, rejoicing, once again addressed himself to those present and murmured these words which concealed whole tons of irony.

"He's trying to take the mickey, this little cuss."

He went on, more severely.

"This little cuss is trying to take the mickey."

And he concluded, absolutely severely:

"In which case, I intend to knock his little block off."

As he was addressing the audience, he had his back half-turned to Pierrot, who judged it prudent to take both the initiative and advantage of the situation. He gave his little car an unexpected kick, thus propelling it into the legs of the threatening fatso. He was hoping thereby to make him lose his balance, after which he intended to take to his heels. He had adopted the rational solution of the famous problem of the two adversaries of disproportionate strength.

The vehicle bore down, then, on the hoofs of the heavyweight, who was still perorating unsuspectingly. The heavyweight toppled over backwards, as foreseen, and landed sprawling, his arms and legs pointing up to heaven, between the seat and the steering wheel. The vehicle pursued its course for another few meters, laden with its involuntary passenger.

Shouts of jubilation came from the rubbernecks. And

Pierrot, instead of making his getaway, stayed where he was, observing the consequences of his valiance with interest. Which enabled a new adversary to rear up in front of him: Monsieur Tortose.

"It's you again!" he exclaimed. "Starting a brawl again!"

Whereupon he perceived that Pierrot's victim, which victim was struggling to his feet, was none other than Eusèbe Pradonet—*Monsieur* Pradonet—the owner of Uni Park.

"Oh!" he said.

And to Pierrot:

"You—I've got some good advice for you: get the hell out, this minute, and don't ever show your face here again. No point in coming back tomorrow. Go on—scram!"

"What about my day's wages, Monsieur Tortose?"

Pradonet came up. Monsieur Tortose, the kindly fellow, handed over two or three little bank notes, and Pierrot, fleeing the proprietorial excoriation, soon found himself back in the darkness, a few meters away from the incandescent entrance to Uni Park. Once again, he was out of a job.

Someone patted him on the shoulder.

"Come on, mate," said Paradis, "don't worry, come and have a drink with us, things'll work out."

But they didn't work out. The next day, in spite of Paradis's—and even Petit-Pouce's—insistence, Tortose, scared of Pradonet, refused to take Pierrot back.

2

FOR MANY YEARS, Pradonet had been in the habit of shaving on the stroke of 5:30–6:00 o'clock, just before the aperitif, so as to look good at dinner and during the whole course of the evening. When he was expecting a guest, he performed this task with even greater care. He was now taking especial pains because, three days before, he had issued a dinner invitation to Crouïa Bey, the fakir who was going to exhibit himself in the Uni Park booth recently occupied by the Aquarium Man, and previously, in ascending chronological order, by the Pithecanthropess, the Belly Dancer, Turlupin the conjurer, and many others.

While he was applying himself to scraping his hide, Léonie, his mistress—who got called Madame Pradonet, even though she was only the widow Prouillot—Léonie was squeezing her curves into an armature ad hoc, not that she was already obese, but well, it was coming, it was coming, and did she not like to appear beautiful? She succeeded, then, in moderating her fleshly expansion and, after this effort, sat down on the edge of the bed, looking pensively at Pradonet's face which she could see reflected in the mirror with one cheek swollen, it being distended the better to slash the hairs. Then his face, relieved of its shaving soap and pilosity, gradually lit up until it became the very picture of joy.

"What are you laughing at?" asked Léonie.

Pradonet, who was still only smiling, opened his cakehole wider and hiccupped a laugh.

"Oh, don't aggravate me," said Léonie.

He didn't stop. She shrugs her shoulders and begins to put her stockings on.

"Don't you know what I'm thinking about?" asked Pradonet, who was calming down.

"What do I care?"

"I was thinking about yesterday evening. What a fool I must have looked, sprawling in my little go-cart. Ha ha ha!"

"I've always thought you were an imbecile," said Léonie. "You have no dignity. If you hadn't had me, you'd have let everybody pull a fast one on you. You wouldn't be the boss of Uni Park, that's for sure. Who's got the most money in this business? Me, haven't I. To please you, I allow people to believe you're an important gentleman. Yes, without me, what'd have become of you? I even wonder whether you'd have been capable of punching the tickets at the gate, you're such a dope. You're a born sucker. If someone came and clouted you, you'd turn the other cheek to get another one."

"I think you're exaggerating there, Léonie. Ah well, in any case I reckon he had me, the little cuss. Ha ha ha!"

"He got the sack, I hope."

"Yes yes, don't worry. Poor boy."

"Was it Tortose who hired him?"

"Yes, he was working at the Palace."

"I know that. I asked you whether it was Tortose or you who hired him."

"It was Tortose."

"There's another one who works wonders. Oh la la, if I wasn't here, what a mess it'd be."

They finished dressing. The doorbell rang.

"Hm, that'll be the fakir," said Léonie. "He's much too early. If you ask me, he didn't have any lunch, so's to shovel it away at our expense. We'll let him cool his heels a bit, that'll teach him."

"He's superb, you know."

"If he wasn't, I wouldn't have hired him."

"Ah no, come on! ah no, come on! I think you're exaggerating there. Even so, you aren't going to tell me that it wasn't me that hired him?"

"In the first place. I'll say whatever I choose, and in the next place, you'd have agreed to ridiculous terms with him if I hadn't nagged you into making the fellow moderate his demands. And in any case, you mustn't kid yourself, you know, because fakirs are terribly out-of-date. He's here because he's cheap. Otherwise . . ."

"What I think, I think they're terrific, these guys who stick pins this long down their gullets. It gives you a splendid idea of man's capacities. That's what *I* think."

"Pah. People turn up their noses at their tricks these days. They won't have them in the music halls any more. He'll last a couple of weeks here at the very most, just time for us to find something else to put in that booth after him."

"*I* shall go and see him. I like that sort of thing."

"You big booby," said Léonie, collapsing into Pradonet's arms.

She came over all lovey-dovey.

"You big baby, my big lambikins, my stupid cabbagehead, my fatuous fat piggy, my numskull, my silly sausage."

There is a knock at the door. The maid wants to know whether they're going to have dinner soon, if not it's all going to be burnt, and if they don't hurry up the guest will have drunk all the Dubonnet, even though he considers this aperitif wishy-washy, to go by what he said under his breath.

"We're coming," said Léonie.

She detached herself from Pradonet, with the sound made by the suction cup of a Eureka dart when it's pulled off the board.

"*Now* what are you smiling at?" she asked.

"I'm still thinking about yesterday evening. It must have been absolutely side-splitting to see me sprawling in my little go-cart. Ha ha ha!"

"What a dimwit," said Léonie.

They got going, and a few instants later entered the salon. With a single glance, Léonie gauges the quantity of Dubonnet absorbed by Crouïa Bey to be the equivalent of the content of five wine glasses. The fakir hastens up to her and bows low, with a slight belch.

"My respects, Madame," he articulates.

He's a knockout, is Crouïa Bey. He has glowing eyes, the forehead of a thinker, the hands of a pianist, a wasp waist, a sapper's beard, lips of coral, the thorax of a bull, ah! isn't he handsome! ah! isn't he handsome!

He hasn't half made a hit with Léonie.

Pradonet and he cordially shake each other's dexter hand.

Yvonne (she's Pradonet's daughter) enters. She is introduced to the fakir.

They are beginning to chat when they are told that dinner is served.

They sit down in the dining room around a lobster mayonnaise, on the subject of which they comment for a short while. Then comes the gigot, inside which are cloves of garlic so big that they might be cooked maggots. This mass of flesh is accompanied by kidney beans; everyone thinks about the wind-breaking that their absorption will provoke, but one either has manners or one has not: hush! no jokes on that subject! Pradonet watches the fakir with admiration. Doesn't he just shovel it in. He's wolfing it down. Léonie was right: it's not possible, he can't have had lunch. As for Léonie, she's forgotten her prognosis. She's observing the guest out of the corner of her eye. He has such fantastic poise. Hell's bells! he's so distinguished! He must be used to feeding in high society. Léonie feels affection for him. She'd like to tease him. As for Yvonne, none of this interests her; as from the previous evening she has a new lover, young Perdrix, who works at The Enchanted River. She gave herself to him in one of the little boats that takes lovers around in a fireproofed cardboard Venice. It was rocking horribly, they were afraid they were going to fall into the water, which was full of dust and ashes. Ah well, they're young, they thought they were getting pleasure out of it. Hence she has other preoccupations than the dinner, the fakir, and all the rest.

"I'll bet," says Léonie, "I'll bet you know He'lem Bey."

He'lem Bey is a famous fakir, a native of Rueil, whose first name is Victor. He's well known all over Paris.

"I?" exclaimed Crouïa Bey, "good gracious no, dear Madame. He'lem Bey? A charlatan, who has brought the profession into disrepute. Personally, I have only ever had dealings with real ones."

"Pah," said Léonie, "are there any real ones, then? Where?"

"Right here, for a start. You only have to look at me."

"What part of the boondocks do you come from, Monsieur Crouïa Bey?" asked Léonie.

"From Tataouïne, in the south of Tunisia," replied the Fakir, making a decisive gash in a cliff of Roquefort. "Ah, Tataouïne, Tataouïne! agi mena, fiça l'arbiya, chouïa chouïa barka, excuse me, it's homesickness that gets me in the guts, nostalgia for the desert . . . for the desert with its camels that sway . . . look, like this."

He stood up and walked round the table, imitating the lolloping gait of the dromedary. Eusèbe and Léonie, throwing themselves back on their chairs, dislocated their jaws, they found this so stupendous.

"Susususususuperb," Pradonet stammered.

Léonie wiped her eyes.

"Joking aside," she said, "I'll bet you come from Houilles or Bezons, maybe even from Sartrouville, I can tell by your accent."

"No, dear Madame," replied the fakir, "I am a real Arab. A real, genuine one. Listen to this."

He gave utterance to the muezzin's call to prayer.

"That's really something," said Pradonet with approval.

"Ah, I've got it," Léonie exclaimed. "You wouldn't by any chance be the brother of Jojo Mouilleminche, would you, the chap who used to sing at the Européen under the name of Chaliaqueue?"

"Oh, be quiet, you can see very well you're annoying him," said Pradonet, seeing Crouïa Bey's face lengthen. "And you," he added, turning to Yvonne, "time to go!"

Without a word, Yvonne rose from the table.

"Is Mademoiselle already leaving us?" said the fakir gallantly.

"Don't keep her back," said Pradonet irritably, "she's got to go to work. It isn't difficult, at that, or particularly tiring, what we ask of her."

Yvonne left the room.

"She has a little stand with a machine gun. It keeps her busy. Until she gets married. Me, I'm not going to keep her in idleness, that's for sure. Even though I could easily afford to, if I wanted."

"I'm sure you could," said the fakir. "With a business like this, you must have a tidy sum stashed away."

"You might say that I'm not one of the people who tremble when they see quarter day coming up. Considering that I'm my own boss!"

"You don't have to tell him the story of your life," said Léonie.

"Pooh! I'm not giving away any secrets. Everyone knows that this dump belongs to me. He might even have been capable of guessing it."

To the fakir:

"Do you go in for second sight?"

"No. You know as well as I do that second sight's all eyewash."

"He gets mental blocks like that," Léonie told him. "He's no genius."

"Personally," Crouïa Bey continued, "my acts are dependable, concrete, real: sabers, hatpins, nailboards, broken glass, live coals. And I don't fake anything."

"Wow," said Pradonet, with conviction.

But Léonie was determined to tease the fakir.

"Are you quite sure," she asked, "that you aren't Jojo Mouilleminche's brother? I remember he was always telling me that after his brother had done his military service in Africa, he stayed there. He'd done all kinds of jobs, and then one day his vocation came to him: he wanted to become a fakir. That wouldn't be you by any chance?"

"Oh, leave him alone," said Pradonet. "Anyone would think this was the Inquisition."

"'T's a fallacy, 't's a fallacy," said Crouïa Bey, "but I can see that Madame is trying to lead me up the garden. Of course I don't know this Jojo What's-his-name."

He swallowed his coffee, boiling hot as was only right, and put his cup down with a meditative gesture that was not lacking in grace. Léonie observed the undulations of his beard which reflected his hesitation between taking the line of the obstinate lie and that of the more or less complete avowal.

"A cigar?" Pradonet suggested.

The fakir accepted, cut its end with precision (and distinction), and lit it with the lighter held out by his host.

"Right," he said. "Right, right," he added. "Right, that's right," he concluded. "Have to admit that it's a strange coincidence."

"I guessed right, then?" asked Léonie.

"You hit the bull's-eye," Mouilleminche replied. "My name is Robert, and my kid brother *was* the singer. You knew him, then? Life certainly is odd. It's a small world! So you knew him?"

"And how," said Léonie. "He was my first flame."

"Doesn't surprise me," said Mouilleminche, "there never was a greater womanizer than him."

"What are you insinuating?" asked Léonie.

"You aren't going to tell me he wasn't sex-mad?" exclaimed Mouilleminche. "Witness the fact that he died of it."

"Is he dead?" exclaimed Léonie.

She hesitated for a moment. But it was obvious that he was dead.

"My first love!" she wailed.

And there were tears. Pradonet went up to her to console her, but she didn't want to be consoled, not she.

"That's smart, telling stories without thinking," he said to the fakir. "It's obvious you *don't* have second sight."

"Oh, leave him be," murmured Léonie. "But he must tell me how it happened."

"I'm quite willing to," said Mouilleminche. "Only you mustn't cry. What can you expect, it happens to everyone, doesn't it? We all have to come to it. And then, me that's his brother, I certainly don't cry for him. True, I'm used to the idea by now: that he's dead."

"Get on with your story, then," said Pradonet. "You can see she'll enjoy hearing it."

But Léonie was gradually returning to a more normal state.

"You must think me absurd," she said to the fakir, dabbing at her eyes. "Getting in such a state for a fellow you knew when you were seventeen and who chucked you at seventeen-and-a-half. Just like I say. I should add that he was the one who initiated me into love. Well then, so he's dead? I'd always wondered what became of him. I didn't see his name on the bills any more. I told myself he must have hit a bad patch and be kicking his heels in the sticks somewhere far away from Paris."

"Well no, it wasn't that. He's dead. And since then, he isn't kicking his heels in the sticks or anywhere else. This is how it happened. He was singing in Palinsac when he fell in love with a girl who was the daughter of a very respectable gentleman in the town. He had, this gentleman, a beautiful house in a suburb, in the middle of a garden surrounded by a big wall, and my brother, who was a daredevil, jumped over the wall, crossed the garden and went into the splendid villa where the girl was waiting for him, and she wasn't short of nerve, either. But believe it or not, one morning he was found stretched out full length at the bottom of the wall, in the road. He'd come a cropper on his way out. His skull was smashed to bits, and no longer usable. That's how my brother died."

"Well that really *is* a death," said Léonie with enthusiasm.

"It's romantic, it's passionate, it's living. My Pradonet wouldn't meet a death like that, would you, my big jellyfish?"

"Hrrmph," said Pradonet.

"And the girl?" Léonie asked. "What became of her?"

"I haven't the slightest idea," the fakir replied. "I couldn't even tell you her name or address. At that time I was in Alexandria, you know, in Egypt. My mother wrote and told me about it, and when I came back to Europe my mother had died, I didn't have any family left, because my father—I never knew him."

"You were an orphan, huh," said Pradonet.

"That Jojo, all the same," said Léonie pensively. "Dying like that: what a business! And it doesn't make us any younger. They were the days, those were, I was young, I didn't give a damn about anything, and I sang. Because I was a singer, Sidi Mouilleminche, a variety singer. I used to prance around in a short, sequinned skirt, you should have seen it. 'So what, he's not my father,' I'd warble, banging my nose with my knee. I had a way of doing high kicks, wow! I was never short of men. And then one day my voice broke; so I got married and took on the paybox at one of the attractions . . . But I've never forgotten Jojo."

"Madame Prouillot is very sentimental," said Pradonet, "whereas me, my first love, oh la la, I'd be totally incapable of saying who she was."

Crouïa Bey raised his brandy glass and, by way of changing the subject:

"Your health," he said.

"Your very good health," said Léonie and Pradonet.

They tossed back the liquor and remained silent for a few instants, sucking their cigars, they: Eusèbe, Robert and Léonie, for the lady dressed in a somewhat mannish fashion and was given to strong tobacco.

"And what do you think of your booth?" Pradonet asked the fakir.

"Not bad. Obviously I've seen better, but times are hard."

"Do you need any assistants?"

"One will be enough. I have a costume for him. Any out-of-work bum will do."

"And you guarantee me six shows between nine and midnight?"

"Haven't I promised?"

"Sure, sure," said Pradonet "Well then, six times an evening you'll lick a bar of white-hot iron?"

"Precisely."

"What *I* wonder," said Léonie, "is who on earth that girl could have been."

"No idea," replied the fakir. "I haven't got anyone at the moment, could you find me someone to hand me my props?"

"We can meet for an aperitif at the Uni Bar tomorrow at noon," said Pradonet, "there's plenty of bums hanging around there."

"Right," said the fakir.

"I must confess that I've known more than one man," said Léonie, "but my goodness, I've never forgotten *him*, so you can understand that she intrigues me, that girl, my Jojo's last mistress."

She drowned the stub of her cigar in the footbath stagnating in her saucer.

"What do you think, Sidi Mouilleminche?" she asked the fakir.

"I've never bothered about it," replied Crouïa Bey wearily.

"If you don't mind my saying so, my love," said Pradonet, "I think that's rather a morbid idea of yours."

"What d'you expect, it's curiosity."

"The Eternal Feminine," sighed the fakir gallantly,

accompanying this remark with his most charming smile. "Eve
. . . Psyche . . . Pandora . . ."

"'Corporal, replied Pandora,'" Pradonet sang softly,
"'Corporal, you are right.'"

"No need to try to make a fool of me with your allusions
that I don't understand," said Léonie. "I'm not stupid, believe
me."

"Darling," said Pradonet, taking her hand tenderly.

They sat there for a few instants, solemnly looking into each
other's eyes. The fakir's beard undulated gently under the effect
of indescribable thoughts.

"Come on, we've got to get to work," said Léonie, abruptly
withdrawing her hand from the adulterous grasp.

She stands up decisively. Crouïa Bey also rises, somewhat
surprised and embarrassed.

"Oh, don't go," said Pradonet. "*We* aren't in a hurry. Léonie
is at her post on the stroke of nine, and . . ."

"You can explain later," says Léonie. "I haven't got time to
wait. Excuse me, Sidi Mouilleminche, but punctuality, you
know, is what helps you make your fortune. I hope we'll meet
again and talk about all this some more. Jojo . . . all the same
. . . Ah well . . . Bye-bye, Zebbi."

Eusèbe and his mistress kissed without circumspection,
and for his part the fakir once again bowed low over an out-
stretched hand, which he observed was copiously diamonded.
He even came close to grazing his nose, which was long, on
an aggressive ten-carat.

Léonie departed, the big boss offered a cigar, another round
of brandy:

"Yes," said he, "that's the way she is. Every evening during the
season, at nine on the dot, she goes and sits beside the Alpinic
Railway cashier and supervises the Park from her observation

post. If something's going wrong, she moves. I must tell you too that the attraction belongs to her: it belonged to her husband when we went into partnership. Didn't you ever know her husband? Alberic Prouillot? A former conjurer who one day broke his fingers on a Negro's jaw, and believe it or not this Negro who came from Martinique and was called Louis Durand, this Negro had a little merry-go-round which he sold, and, as Prouillot could no longer practice his profession, they went into partnership and bought the Alpinic Railway which was brand-new in those days, I'm talking about fifteen or so years ago, I've modernized it since. Then Durand died, and when I founded Uni Park it was with Prouillot alone. Mind you, I'm not saying that Prouillot was my only partner, because you need capital to set up a business like this, I'm simply saying that at that time the Alpinic belonged to Prouillot alone. But my stories are boring you, eh?"

"Not in the least."

"Well . . . all I can tell you is that the Jojo in question, your brother that is, I never knew him. In those days I wasn't even thinking about Léonie, for the very good reason that I didn't even know she existed. It's true. I owned a children's dobby horse merry-go-round, real wooden horses they were, that I'd inherited from my father, it wasn't up to much, I can tell you. I started from more or less nothing, that's for sure, but would you like to see what I've become? Come with me."

He emptied his glass with the same decision Léonie had shown in knocking hers back, and stood up.

"We'll go up on to the terrace," he went on, "and I'll show you."

The fakir gulped down the last drops of the quantity of alcohol his host had allotted him.

"Excellent, this brandy."

"You enjoyed your dinner, then?" Pradonet asked cordially. "Good. Well then, you are now about to contemplate one of those points of view—just you wait!"

So he led his guest on to the terrace of the block of flats he had had built at one of the angles of the quadrilateral occupied by Uni Park, at the corner of the Boulevard Extérieur and the Avenue de la Porte d'Argenteuil. The three of them, Pradonet, his daughter, and Madame Prouillot, lived on the two top floors. The Tortoses lived on the second, the Perdrixs on the first, and the concierges on the ground floor, plus any chance guests, who occupied ad hoc rooms from time to time.

"What d'you think of that, then?" Pradonet asked, when they had arrived.

Uni Park lay spread out beneath them, luminous, populous and sonorous. Music, sounds and shouts rose up all together; they assailed the ears en bloc. Above the multiple lights, whether stationary or moving, aeroplanes attached to a tall pylon were silently revolving in a zone that was already dark, and hence poetic. But beneath, everything looked very like a cheese crawling with black larvae lit up by glowworms.

"Well," said Pradonet, "all that belongs to me, or as good as. In any case, I control, I command, I organize. I won't tell you my turnover, but there are days when we see a hundred thousand visitors. Twenty attractions share them turn and turn about, and I'm not counting the tombolas, the games of skill and the shooting galleries that you can see, most of them grouped together, down there between the Alpinic Railway and the Palais de Danse, by the gate at the corner of the Avenue de Chaillot and the Rue des Larmes. But the main entrance is down there in front of us, the one at the corner of the Boulevard Extérieur and the Avenue de Chaillot, and on the right as you come in, on our left, that is, do you recognize the booth I've earmarked for you? Just in front of the Métro Fantastique, where the crowd's gathering?"

"I do," said Crouïa Bey.

"Yes. All that. All that belongs to me. Or as good as. And I started from nothing. Or as good as: a dobby horse merry-go-round, real wooden horses, my dear sir."

"And that dark part there: what's that?"

"Where d'you mean?"

"But there . . . along that road . . . it looks as if there's a little chapel, and some trees . . ."

"Oh, that? that's nothing. Doesn't belong to me. We'll go down now, if that's all right with you."

"Hm, do you go in for astronomy?" asked the fakir, spotting a telescope mounted on a tripod.

"Oh, that? I sometimes use it to keep an eye on the proceedings. Here, would you like to see Madame Prouillot at the Alpinic Railway paybox?"

He swivelled the spyglass. The fakir put his eye to it.

"Yes, she's there all right," he said politely.

Pradonet then put his own eye to it.

"Good old Léonie," he murmured, "reliable as ever, but she's feeling melancholy this evening. It's your Jojo's fault," he added, turning to the fakir.

"If she hadn't insisted, though, we wouldn't have talked about him."

"Quite true. Women, all the same, they're queer fish. Never think like everyone else. We men, things run smoothly, whereas with them, it's all fits and starts. But you have to admit that their monthlies have something to do with it. They mess up the way their minds work, because there's a connection between them, that's my opinion. And anyway, you must have studied that to be able to do your stunts, you must know the human body."

Pradonet oriented his instrument in a different direction.

"Here, would you like to see my daughter?"

The fakir put his eye to it.

"Yes, she's there all right," he said politely.

Pradonet then put his own eye to it.

"That would have been all we needed," he said. "Can you imagine, yesterday she ditched the whole outfit and went and got herself treated to a ride on the bumper cars by a young fancy-pants, and I certainly wonder what he might have had that appealed to her. The bitch isn't hard to please, I know that, but even so, work's work. You don't just leave your stand like that. Because for the rest, I don't have any illusions: she isn't worth much. It's the times we live in: the papers have warned us."

He sighs, and once again changes the orientation of his glass.

"Now," says he, "we'll take a little look at the entrances and see what the trade's like."

"Go ahead," says the fakir, who's had his bellyful of Parkoscopy.

Pradonet attaches an eye.

"It's all right, there's plenty of movement. Hullo. . ."

"Is something wrong?" asked the fakir.

"Hullo hullo . . . but it's my young reprobate . . ."

Still half bent over, he turned round to Crouïa Bey:

"It's the lad who debauched my daughter yesterday, and who afterwards, I simply must tell you this, and who afterwards pushed a dodgem car into my legs and I went sprawling into it. If it'd been anyone but me I'd have found it no end comical. The lad was working at the Palace; after that business they gave him the push, natürlich. Well, I've just seen him come in again. He'd paid the entrance fee, I saw him pocket his ticket. He's stopped in front of your poster."

Once again he put his eye to the eyepiece.

"Shit!" he exclaimed, "he's disappeared."

He began to pursue him, training his telescope in all directions. He finally caught up with him.

"Ah, there he is again. In front of The Big Green Snake. No, that doesn't interest him. Now he's going over to the Palais de Danse, but he surely doesn't intend to go in. Just as I thought, he's going on past it. Now he's in front of a tombola, it almost looks as if he's going to play, but no, he's content to watch the wheel go round. He's had enough. He's off. There he is in front of The Sleeping Beauty, now that's an attraction invented by Prouillot. There's a woman in bed, you know, twenty sous entitle you to aim at a target, and if you hit the bull's-eye the bed tips up and you can see the bird roll over on to the ground. She's undressed, I don't need to tell you that. It rakes the money in, an attraction like that. He was no fool, Prouillot. But my young fellow's going on. I know where he's going, my young fellow. Naturally. Didn't I say so. There he is, chatting her up again. What a nerve he's got. And what on earth can he be saying to her?"

"You don't mind if I come and have a bit of a chat with you?" Pierrot asked Yvonne.

"Of course not," Yvonne replied. "On the contrary, it's nice of you to come and see me again."

"You didn't get into trouble after the business yesterday?"

"The traditional bawling-out, mostly because I ditched the stand."

"So, no kidding, you're the big boss's daughter?"

"Why wouldn't I be?"

"Even so," said Pierrot, "he's quite somebody."

"Come off it, you needn't try to put me down. I don't take myself for Lady Muck."

"And you work, just like that?"

"Have to. It's orders. And anyway, I don't mind. I see people. I'm getting my educaaaation."

"You're a laugh. You don't seem to give a damn."

"You've got the blue devils, haven't you? this evening."

"Well, it isn't funny. I haven't got a job. I'm still one of the unemployed."

"Poor thing. They gave you the push, it's rotten."

"Pah! And you, you really didn't have any problems?"

"No no—as you see."

"And it's going well tonight?"

"So-so."

A group of kids approached.

"Don't be scared," said Pierrot. "It's forty sous for twenty-five shots and you'd think you were in Chicago. And then, it gets you in training for war. Don't hesitate, lads, it's a unique opportunity."

One of the boys stepped up with his deuce, and during that time he and Yvonne continued their conversation.

"Papa seems to be a holy terror," said Pierrot.

"Don't you believe it. To my mind he isn't terrible at all. When you're the boss, though, you've got to kick up a row."

"Maybe. The lady with him, *she* can't be easy. She was looking daggers at him."

"After all, what's it got to do with you?"

"Oh! nothing. I was just chatting."

"Let's chat about something more amusing."

"You must excuse me."

"You're already excused, don't worry."

The kid had filled his target. Yvonne went and got it for him.

"Not up to much, chum," said Pierrot, "Have to have another go."

The boy allowed himself to be persuaded, and once again the machine gun crackled.

"Well then," said Pierrot to Yvonne, "couldn't we see each other somewhere a bit quieter one of these days?"

"It's difficult. I'm here all afternoon and all evening."

"And after that?"

"How you do go on."

"When then? In the morning?"

"Perhaps."

"Where?"

"Hold on. Not so fast."

"Then you don't want to?"

"I said perhaps in the morning."

"Where?"

"I sometimes go down the Rue des Larmes around eleven. But don't wait for me any longer. If you don't see me, it's that I won't have been able to."

"Where is it, this Rue des Larmes?"

"The street behind, the one that runs from the side entrance to the Avenue de la Porte d'Argenteuil."

"Will you be there tomorrow?"

"Perhaps."

"*I* shall be there."

The loader was empty. Yvonne went and fetched the target. Then Pierrot felt he had wings: two muscle-men had each just grabbed him by an arm and were whisking him towards the exit with such velocity that his heels didn't touch the ground, and with such great skill that nobody noticed his disappearance. Waiting for him near the paybox were two other hefties, who gave him some dirty looks. They said to each other:

"Will you recognize his mug? Yes? Right then: not allowed to let him in again."

Then all four of them heaved him out into the night.

"Nice work, that," said Pradonet, who had been following the scene from the heights of his terrace. "You saw how I go about things? A phone call, and hup! the troublemaker's out with no disturbance and no casualties. That's organization for you. Don't you agree?"

"Splendid," said the fakir.

"Poor devil," added Pradonet. "He's certainly unfortunate. Can you imagine, though, coming and disturbing the employees when they're working. Yvonne has better things to do than listen to his blarney. He's unlucky. You can see that at once. For instance, he might well not have been noticed this evening. But no! he had to get himself spotted: and by me, what's more! Do you believe in luck. Monsieur Mouilleminche, you who know such a lot of things?"

"It's something that can be controlled, like everything else."

"No!" exclaimed Pradonet. "You aren't going to tell me that . . . when a flowerpot falls on your head, for example . . ."

"Fakirs never get hit on the head by flowerpots."

Dreamily, Pradonet put away his spyglass.

"And that part that isn't lit up!" Crouïa Bey asked, "you haven't told me what it is."

"Yes I have," replied Pradonet tetchily. "I told you it was nothing. Nothing. Nothing."

3

PIERROT HAD BEEN LIVING in the same hotel for the last two years, it had become a habit, the Hôtel de l'Aveyron, a flimsily-built, single-storeyed edifice with an exterior balcony by means of which each room could communicate with the others. The courtyard was a former farmyard; a little window looked out onto a convent garden. His neighbor was an extremely discreet and silent old workman. Farther off there were couples who mainly minded their own business. The owners were indifferent. A sluttish maid had never made any attempts on Pierrot's virtue. And in any case, she was a decent sort, and quite obliging. Pierrot felt very much at home in these lodgings.

The day after his second expulsion from Uni Park he didn't get up until quite late, around seven, after having a nice lie in. He carefully washed all those places that are liable to smell, moistened his hair, brushed himself down with his hand, wiped his shoes on the bottom of his trousers, he's ready, now he's standing at a counter in front of a boiling hot cup of coffee, he's reading *La Veine*, seeking the nice little nag on which he'll risk a couple of finifs, he'll consider the matter all morning, it isn't eight yet.

He's back in his room. The floor has been swept and the bed made. Pierrot spreads *La Veine* out on it. so's not to dirty the bedspread, then lies down. He smokes. He's waiting for the hours to pass. The men have gone to work. The housewives are gossiping. Cars are going by in the street, little girls are playing in the convent garden. It's all very calm.

From time to time Pierrot closes his eyes, and that way he skips ten minutes or a quarter of an hour. When he reopens his eyes, everything's the same. So he starts waiting again, he has another cigarette, and once again occasional, leisurely puff-puffs of smoke drift halfway up to the ceiling. A big sunbeam is lying in front of the door, which is open onto the balcony. Big flies come in and circle around the room, then go out again, irritated. Small ones are mooching about all over the place. The housewives have gone shopping. The children's recreation is over. The traffic is humming no more than a stone's throw away. Everything has changed, everything will change again, with the hours.

At half past nine Pierrot gets up, folds *La Veine*, and is on his way. It's a good step from his hotel to Uni Park; he did it on foot. He walked without haste, never raising his soles very far above the asphalt. He stopped in front of the shops that took his fancy: the property sellers with their villas in the country, the stamp sellers, the bicycle sellers, the newspaper sellers, the garages. He never missed the window of a manufacturer of ball bearings, with its display of little steel spheres mathematically rebounding on drums made of the same metal. Then he went up the Avenue de Chaillot, and soon caught a glimpse of Uni Park: its monumental entrance gate with its naked women modeled in stucco, their chignons, their broad pelvises and their abdominal ptoses, the framework of the Alpinic Railway, the aeroplane tower.

Still without haste, he passed the closed gates, walked along the wall of the Palais de Danse, and then at the corner of the Rue des Larmes turned right, by the side entrance, whose gates were also closed.

Until then he had never been in this street, which was almost in the shantytown area. Its left bank was occupied by car repair shops and a few bistros, as well as a villa which must have dated from the days of Louis Philippe. On the other side, the Uni Park wall stopped short some twenty meters from the Avenue de Chaillot. Farther on, separated from the road by an iron gate, was a sort of chapel in the middle of a sort of square. At first. Pierrot took no interest in it. He walked up and down, watching for Yvonne to appear at either end. But Yvonne did not appear. When noon arrived, he could only think that she would not come that day.

Pierrot then noticed a man coming out of the Louis Philippe house; locking it behind him; crossing the road; with a second key opening the iron gate; going into the square; with a third key opening the door of the chapel, it did indeed seem to be a chapel, but of a style unknown to Pierrot, who in any case was not much of an archeologist. And this is where the man enters. The door closes behind him. Pierrot is interested, and begins to wonder whether he won't risk a few steps in that direction. Which he finally does. But the man comes out at this moment. And Pierrot:

"Excuse me, Monsieur, could you tell me . . ."

But the man:

"Are you a Poldevian, young man?"

"Me? No. And besides, I don't know what . . ."

"What then? Just curious?"

"Well, I happened to be passing, and . . ."

"Aha, young man! you mean you don't know what this chapel is?"

"Not at all, Monsieur."

"Aha! it is indeed not a very well-known monument. There are quite a few books that mention it, but they are very scholarly, and only to be found in libraries."

"I've never had much time to spend in libraries."

"I'm not reproaching you, young man. So you were wondering what it might be?"

"Yes, Monsieur. If I'm not being indiscreet . . ."

"Not at all. But . . ."

He pulled a beautiful turnip out of his pocket and looked at the time.

". . . it's lunch time. I'll tell you another day. Goodbye, young man."

And he crossed the road. Opening the door of his house with his first key, he went in.

Outside a garage, some workmen were chatting. Pierrot went up to them and made polite inquiries as to the origins and nature of the little monument to be seen over there, in the square.

"No idea," said one.

"Actually, what's it got to do with you?" said another.

"It's a chapel," replied a third. "To visit it, you have to apply to the chap who lives opposite."

"Is that so!" said the first two, blinded by this science.

They began to examine the thing, which up till then they had never noticed.

Pierrot thanked them for the information, and then made for the Uni Bar, a café that was famous in the district, at the corner of the Avenue de la Porte d'Argenteuil and the Boulevard Extérieur, opposite Pradonet's block of flats. The Uni Park employees flocked there; it had a tobacco counter and ran a pari-mutuel, which attracted additional customers; it served as an observation and information post for the women who solicited around (and thanks to) the attractions; its sandwiches were good. Pierrot orders one, a ham one, with butter and plenty of mustard, and according to custom washes it down with white wine. He was hoping to meet Paradis, but didn't find him. So, still biting into his lunch, he went up to the pari-mutuel employee's cage. It was too late. Pierrot knew it. He looked for his horse on the list, and didn't too greatly regret not having backed it. He fell back on a pinball machine, and put twenty sous in the money-minter. He soon had a circle around him, and it was an admiring circle. It was marvelous to see the little balls succeed in traveling along the maximum itineraries, find their way into the runways that were the best defended by the most ingenious obstacles, drop into the cups, light up the markers, bump into the pins. Pierrot notched up twenty-two thousand points in his first game, namely seven thousand more than he needed to entitle him to a free game. The second time he reaches thirty thousand; the third, he's down to sixteen thousand; the fourth, he climbs up again to thirty-one thousand. All that for twenty sous. He'd finished his sandwich; he graciously abandoned his free game to a nondescript kid who wouldn't be afraid to make himself ridiculous by manipulating the machine after him.

"Well, my boy, you seem to know all the tricks!"

Pierrot thought he recognized his interlocutor; he wasn't sure. He drank his white wine without haste, and then:

"One does one's best," he said modestly.

"You do your best, too, when you send your bloody boss sprawling," Pradonet retorted.

"How much is that?" Pierrot asked the waiter.

"Mustn't run away, I'm not going to hurt you. Ha ha! what a trick you played on me the other day! Ha ha!"

Pierrot pocketed his change and couldn't quite see how to escape.

"I recognize you all right." Pradonet insisted, "I'm eagle-eyed. And what are you doing now?"

"I'm on the loose," said Pierrot resolutely.

Pradonet examined him for a few moments in silence, and then:

"You make me feel a bit ashamed, you know."

He turned to an individual, as bearded as he was distinguished, who was hanging around behind him:

"Here," he said, "here's a boy who'll do for you."

"All right," said Crouïa Bey, "but he'll have to take his glasses off."

"What sort of a job is it?" Pierrot asked.

"You'll be dressed as an Indian," said the fakir, "I have a costume, and you hand me the props, with signs of respect. I'll show you. And I'll tan your skin, too."

"That suit you?" Pradonet asked. "You'll be working in the second booth on the right after the paybox."

"Be there this evening at eight," said Crouïa Bey.

"But they won't let me in," said Pierrot.

"I'll give orders," said Pradonet. "But don't start chatting my daughter up again. If you do—watch out! Off the premises, that's your business, I couldn't care less. But in working hours, you have to behave."

"Thank you very much, Monsieur," said Pierrot.

"See you this evening then," said Crouïa Bey.

"How much will I be given?" asked Pierrot.

"Ten francs an evening," said Crouïa Bey.

"The whole evening?" asked Pierrot.

"Yes," said Crouïa Bey.

"Twenty francs, then," said Pierrot.

Pradonet began to laugh.

"He's got nerve," he exclaimed.

And to the fakir:

"Go on then, let him have fifteen."

"I don't want to argue," said Crouïa Bey, "but that reduces my profit. I'll do it for *you*."

And to Pierrot:

"All right, fifteen francs. See you this evening, eight o'clock."

The two men departed; Pradonet full of joy, the fakir somewhat displeased.

Pierrot left after them, to keep his distance. He went back to the Rue des Larmes, looked at the house, at the chapel, but didn't dare pass them again. Then he felt inclined to see the Seine, and made his way in that direction. He walked nonchalantly, as was his wont, and was thinking less about his new situation than about the meaning of the little monument.

A few meters away from the toll house he passed an old café inside which there was no doubt a billiard table on its last legs; on the terrace, which consisted of two or three iron tables surrounded by a few wicker chairs, he saw his old man, who was drinking a half. He went up to him.

"Well well," said the guardian from the Rue des Larmes, "were you looking for me, young man?"

"No, not at all," said Pierrot. "I just happened to be . . ."

"But it looks as though you are somehow glad to meet me like this."

"I would find it difficult to say the contrary, but . . ."

"Sit down then, young man."

Pierrot sat down. A housewife came and asked him what he would like to drink; the old-timer rapidly finished his half; two more were ordered.

"Your curiosity has given you flair," the old man said. "You ferreted me out right away."

"But I assure you I wasn't looking for you . . ."

"Come come, don't deny it. And anyway, how would that make you indiscreet? Importunate, at the very most . . ."

Pierrot stood up:

"I wouldn't want you to think . . ."

"Sit down then."

And Pierrot sat down.

"Sit down then: I'm going to tell you my life story."

"But . . . the chapel? . . ." Pierrot asked.

"Listen, and don't interrupt me."

He coughed three times, and uttered these words:

"I was born in the house you saw in the Rue des Larmes, in which I still live. In those days, the Rue des Larmes was only a path which was practically impassable in winter, and Uni Park didn't yet exist. Around us there was nothing but waste ground, little workshops, sheds or stables, shanties, insalubrious businesses, knackers' yards, farms, and even meadows. The district had a bad name; you sometimes found women in little pieces, and informers who had been executed. We used to barricade ourselves in in the evenings, and my father had a gun. I several times heard screams in the night: enough to make you shudder. And I couldn't sleep.

"My father was a big, bony fellow, about six foot tall, and the last representative of an old family from Argenteuil; at one moment he found himself in possession of most of the land between the fortifications and the Seine, on this side of Paris, and the piece of ground on which Uni Park now stands even belonged to him in his own right. To my father. He was what these days would be called a loser. That didn't stop him being happy, I think, despite, of course, some regrets. He had thought himself an artist, he had wanted to become a painter, he only succeeded in fathering a child on a grisette, my mother, who later became an excellent wife, a very timid, modest creature. That was how I knew her, and that was how I saw her die.

"After kicking his heels for some time, my father finally took up a profession: working in wax. He supplied traveling exhibitions and anatomy museums with his art. He was the most highly thought-of modeler in the whole of Paris: he produced perfect likenesses and no one was more skilled than he in using his material to reproduce the particularities of physiognomies or the aberrations of organs or the dilapidations of the flesh. I told you just now that in my childhood there was nothing reassuring about this district, but at home it was even worse. Even though I never went into my father's workshop, from time to time, in unexpected places, I would come across rigid heads which threatened me with their enamel eyes, or unspeakable objects which upset my digestion. And when I was in bed and heard incoherent lamentations or hopeless appeals, I felt that this newly-dead man, dripping with his own blood, was going to force his way into our house and conduct the abominable choir of the waxworks. I sweated with anguish in my bed.

"And so, when I was thirteen, I made every effort to persuade my parents to bind me as an apprentice. I was happy to leave this desolate place, but where I went I found much worse things, of a different description. You can't imagine what the life of an apprentice was like half a century ago, or how atrocious an existence which was already hard for workmen could be for fifteen-year-old children. How I regretted the lonely spots stagnating within a few meters of the fortifications. But it was too late; I had to go on putting up with the bullying, working till I dropped, and dying of hunger. And so my military service, what a holiday! What wonderful memories! Friends . . . travel . . . I did my time in Algeria, young man, and in the Zouaves, what's more . . . a fine regiment: I almost signed on again. And then at the last moment I was overcome with homesickness. I came home.

"During my absence, the neighborhood had changed very little. There were more shanties and gardens, and fanatics were discovering that sports could be played on the waste ground. At the corner of the Avenue de Chaillot there was a ratodrome which catered to the tastes of a clientele of boys, dog lovers and the rich. But at night, all this retreated into taciturn distress, and there was nothing but the sound of murder victims calling for help to distract one's attention from the intensity of the silence. Our old house was still there: I was never again to leave it. I learned the paternal trade; I was a man, and I'd seen worse; what was more, my father had given up making anatomical models and begun to specialize in lifelike dummies. I have been working in this branch up till now, and I still maintain the paternal reputation.

"My father, I don't need to tell you, was of a saturnine, melancholic temperament, a temperament that he has partially bequeathed to me. It may be that a solar or mercurian influence at the very beginning, when I was a child, prevented me from rejoicing at the sight of fleecy cysts or suppurating chancres. But it is a fact that at a very early age I came to like solitude, the secluded life, my pipe, the company of brothel women when the urge drives you there; in short, celibate habits. I never married, even though I did several times love a woman with some violence: an Arabian dancer for whom I nearly became a muslim; later, a young girl who worked in a pork butcher's shop in the Avenue de Chaillot; those girls' skin, you know, has a special quality. But finally, neither this one, nor that one, nor any others, made me want her company until the end of all my days on earth.

"My father died a few months after my mother. And that was when I was able to appreciate, to relish the joys and sorrows of the solitary life; but I repeat, I never married. I have also told you that my family owned all this part of the outskirts, right down to the Seine. By the time my father had become the sole representative of the family, all that remained to him was our house, on one side of the road, and on the other side the quadrilateral now occupied by Uni Park—and by the chapel. You may have noticed that the ground round the chapel is in the form of a very elongated rectangle; it is the site of a vegetable garden that my father had kept for himself there. Shortly after his death, a fellow came and asked me to sell him what ground I still possessed. I hesitated. He was offering me what was a considerable sum at the time. I gave in, but I kept the vegetable garden for myself and I promised him I'd reserve it for him when I was thinking of getting rid of it. Life went on as before, the only difference being that I had a little money and didn't have to worry about my old age, because I invested my money in sound French and foreign securities. As for my garden, we continued to cultivate it.

"Well then, one fine morning while I was hoeing my lettuces (I had a particularly fine patch that year—that was not quite twenty years ago and I'd just passed my fiftieth birthday)—it was June, the harsh, blood-red sun above the slates had only just risen over the roofs of Paris, a very thin mist was dancing over by the Bois de Boulogne—I heard a horse galloping, and then a loud cry. My field was surrounded by a little wooden fence. The animal came crashing into it, having shied at goodness knows what, and its rider, following its momentum, dropped like a meteor into the middle of my vegetable garden.

"He didn't move.

"I rushed up. He had fainted. He looked half-dead. I called

for help. Some neighbors came running. They went to fetch a doctor, the police, and later an ambulance. They took the injured man away. In the meantime, he had regained consciousness and wanted to go home. The next day, the papers informed me that he had died there shortly afterwards. They also informed me that he was Prince Luigi Voudzoï, a Poldevian prince who was completing his studies in France. A malicious gossip columnist claimed that these studies consisted mainly of drinking bouts and bacchanalia.

"The funeral took place a few days later. I went to it. It was very beautiful and picturesque; and, what's more, moving. Prince Luigi was buried in Père Lachaise, and when the ceremony was over I stayed until nightfall, dreaming in that district which dominates our capital. I resumed my hoeing. But even while cultivating my garden, I couldn't help thinking about that accident: it was the most important event of my life, it and the time I spent with the Zouaves in North Africa. It had made me famous in the district, and several times a day I found myself having to describe the events I had witnessed. I soon began to feel a desire to know more about the history of the Poldevians who, according to the papers, were the original inhabitants of their distant, mountainous region. I borrowed books from the Argenteuil public library, and I discovered that history could not be understood without a knowledge of chronology and geography, which to me did not seem comprehensible without astronomy and cosmography, nor astronomy and cosmography without geometry and arithmetic. So I began my education again ab ovo, which means from the beginning in the Latin tongue (but it's much more rapid and expressive—you see, young man, the advantages of education). At the end of a few months I had learned or relearned the rules governing the agreement of participles, the way to calculate compound interest, the crucial dates in French history, the departments

with their chief towns and sub-prefectures, the position of the
Great Bear, and a few long speeches from our classics.

"I spent the summer and part of the autumn in this way,
then. One day, when I was sitting outside my front door taking
advantage of the setting sun, I saw a very well-dressed young
gentleman who seemed to be looking for something. He came
up to me and asked me very politely whether I could not show
him exactly the precise spot where a noble foreigner had per-
ished of a violent death a few months previously. 'Nothing is
easier,' I told him, 'for I was the one and only witness of the
accident. It is opposite,' I added, 'in that little vegetable garden you see before you and which is my property.' 'Would it
not be possible for you to conduct me to the very place?' he
asked me. He hastened, moreover, to declare that if this would
in any way inconvenience me, he would come back another
day. And he begged me, finally, to believe that it was not out
of idle curiosity that he had come to request me to go to this
slight trouble; he had valid reasons for doing so, and, in order
to convince me, he stated his name and rank, which he judged
sufficient, and it was. Indeed, I had before me a Poldevian
prince. 'Prince,' I replied, 'I shall not hesitate for an instant to
fulfill this pious duty,' and I led him to the lettuce patch where
the rider had fallen. Two modest wooden crosses marked the
position of his head and of his feet; I had wished in this way
to preserve the memory of this noteworthy occurrence. The
prince was touched by this attention, and wiped away a tear
with his finger. Then he stood in prayer and remained lost in
contemplation for a few moments. Next he made a gesture
indicating that we should withdraw, and left with a profoundly
preoccupied air. I respected his silence, and remained in what
you might call a state of moral attention until he once again
wished to address me. Which he did in these terms:

"'If I have understood you correctly,' he said, 'this vegetable garden belongs to you?' 'Yes, Prince,' I replied. 'You are also the owner of the land?' 'Yes, Prince,' I replied. 'Would you be kind enough to remind me of your name?' 'Artheme Mounnezergues,' I replied. 'And you live? . . .' 'Opposite, Prince,' I replied, 'at number eight, Chemin de la Tuilerie.' 'And you saw Prince Luigi's accident?' 'Yes, Prince,' I replied, 'and I was its only witness.' He then asked me to tell him what I had seen that day. I did so immediately, with great pleasure. The prince listened to me reverently, and when I had come to the end of my account, he assured me that the Poldevian princes would not forget the rare quality of the sentiments evidenced by the two crosses I had planted in my garden. He simply added these two words: 'thank you,' and stepped into a barouche which had no doubt brought him but which I had not noticed. They drove off.

"This visit made me only more eager to pursue my studies, in order to learn more about the Poldevian people and their princes. It also revived my memories, and it did not take me long to perceive that the spot I had marked was of its own accord showing itself to be fateful. The plants around it withered, the slugs that ventured onto it died despairing, and I found the remains of some torrefied caterpillars. Then, when this rough demonstration had been more or less established, I observed that this place was different from every other, and that one always felt there was the shadow of an abstract idea floating over it, the shadow of an event. At night, I could see my field from my bedroom, and although I never saw a silvery ghost walking there in the moonlight, I told myself that never, no never again would I be able to grow carrots and turnips, lettuces or cucumbers in it. And I remained perplexed.

"Years passed. A very long time after the visit I have just described, I was honored to receive a singular missive. I was no little surprised, that morning, to hear the postman invite me to receive a letter. No one ever wrote to me, in fact. This letter was of a large format, written on thick paper, and furthermore, sealed with the Poldevian arms: Sable with eight teardrops argent in orle. I immediately guessed who had sent it. I was invited to go to a certain hotel in the Latin Quarter the next day at around five o'clock. I went. After suffering a most vexatious examination by the hall porter, I was told the number of the room. It was very small and dark; the prince was lying on his bed, smoking. By his side there was the gleam of a bottle, with two glasses. He gestured to me to sit down by him in an armchair, and with his own hand he himself poured me a large quantity of the raki he was drinking. This reminded me of North Africa, but I didn't dare ask him whether he knew that country; that would have been much too familiar. But I listened to my host. 'Monsieur,' he said to me in substance, 'the Poldevian princes have decided to have a chapel built on the very place where Luigi met his death. We wish to erect a permanent memorial to this sad event, and for this purpose, as you have at once understood, it is necessary that this ground, which at present belongs to you, should become our property. I am therefore authorized to ask you at what price you would agree to part with your vegetable garden.' After the thoughts about the fateful place that I had been having at the time and which I imparted to you just now, you will not be surprised to hear that I was not astonished by this proposition. I will even add that it came as a sort of relief to me. But I had to honor my previous commitments. I tried to explain to my interlocutor the obstacle I might see in the fact that I had reserved such a sale to the purchaser of my other land. The prince hastened to dispel my scruples. Was this not a kind of force majeure? Could one weigh the respectable desire of Poldevian princes against the mechanical fulfillment of a contract which was not even a contract, since it was no more than a promise, not even a promise, merely an advance notice, a notification? Was I going to create difficulties for the execution of an act of piety under the idle pretext of satisfying the rapacity of a proprietor desirous of rounding off his land? I was not, was I?

"I agreed, then, to sell my ground, but I soon perceived that my visitor was in no position to conclude the affair there and then. He suggested a payment spread over many years, which would at the same time recompense me for the troubles and worries I might incur in my guardianship of the chapel they were proposing to erect. We finally agreed on a life annuity.

"The building work was immediately put in hand, and in less than six months a chapel had been built. Then they exhumed Prince Luigi from Pere Lachaise, where he had been reposing until then, and buried him in the chapel.

"Thanks to the sale of the land I had inherited and to the annuity the Poldevian princes paid me, I was able to continue my studies, which I orientated mainly towards ancient and modern history, physical and political geography, pure and applied mathematics, the principal dead and living languages, the physical and natural sciences, rhetoric, and theology.

"I had two or three pleasant years. Then, all of a sudden, Uni Park was born, with the violence of its noises, the insolence of its clamors. It was a disgrace, I told myself, to locate an amusement park so near to a tomb. I went to see the director, who was already Pradonet. He, on the contrary, considered it lugubrious and distressing to be in such close proximity to this cemetery that had such a limited purpose. He suggested buying back the land and returning Prince Luigi to Père Lachaise. I refused. He lost his temper. I left him. Since then he has several times made me the same proposition, which I have always rejected, even though in the meantime the situation had changed radically. Indeed, two or three years after the chapel was built, the Poldevian princes stopped paying me my annuity. No one even knew any longer where they were, who they were. In that way I once again became the owner of the field, at the same time as I remained the guardian of the tomb.

"And that's my story, and that of the chapel. What is it? The mausoleum of a Poldevian prince who has neither descendants nor vassals. Who am I? A faithful guardian, who has no explanation. One more detail: if the street I live in is now called the Rue des Larmes, it's because the municipality wanted to pay homage to the Poldevian princes whose coat of arms bears these natural figures in orle."

Mounnezergues finished his half.

"Thank you very much, Monsieur," said Pierrot, "for your illuminating explanations, but I assure you that it was not out of idle curiosity that . . . nor out of selfish curiosity . . . no . . ."

"I understand. There is nothing I subscribe to more than chance . . . or destiny . . . Twenty years ago there was nothing to enable anyone to foresee that the waste ground or the little gardens I saw from my window would become the site for those bizarre, blaring constructions that constitute Uni Park, or that I should snatch from their invading cancer a little strip of land under which, in precarious peace, would lie the noble young victim of a tragic accident. Even less would I have suspected this destiny when, as a Zouave in my baggy trousers, I counted the stars in the Algerian sky during my nights on watch; and, even before that, when I was a child, terrorized by wax models and lost souls, no Sibyl revealed to me that my old age would keep watchful vigil over the sepulcher of a Poldevian."

Pierrot, looking pensive, seemed to acquiesce. His glass was empty.

"Another?" Mounnezergues suggested.

"No, thank you very much, Monsieur. I must go. I have some things to do in the neighborhood . . ."

Mounnezergues was indulgent towards white lies. He paid for the drinks, after Pierrot had made a few modest attempts, and allowed him to continue on his way to wherever he thought fit. Pierrot thanked the old man once again, and they parted, the one returning home, the other going towards the Seine.

On this side, it is no more than a ten-minute walk from the fortifications, from which it is separated by an area of factories producing coffee grinders, others making aeroplanes, and workshops in which unusual makes of cars are repaired. The broad, straight avenue is only paved here and there. Weeds grow, while engines drone. The main artery is the Avenue de Chaillot, which is parallel; this is flowing quite calmly. At its end, there is the river with its barges and its anglers.

Pierrot continued on his way and thought about nothing, which he managed to do with some facility, and even without meaning to; in this way he reached the embankment. On the left, the Chaillot bridge led to Argenteuil, which climbed all the way up the hill. He could hear the roar of the traffic on the main road. The river bank was covered with vigorous, dusty plants. An angler was tempting the fish in a quiet corner. Pierrot sat down and lit a cigarette. He watched the motionless straw hats, and the lines following the current, then smartly leapt back a few meters. A sewer was disgorging its slimy, stained contents into the depths of the running water; people had a predilection for these waters because the fish were no doubt less rare. Some fanatics were riveted in some green boats.

None of this was of any particular interest to Pierrot, although he didn't in the least despise either this spectacle or its elements; nor was he seeking entertainment, and he soon came round to contemplating his mental picture of Yvonne.

Since the age of twelve, Pierrot had been in love a hundred times, quite often successfully so. But Yvonne—he considered her very different, and his love quite new, with an unknown flavor and original possibilities. Even though his experience was fairly vast, ranging from the big-hearted prostitute to the charming shop girl and the come-hither little bit of fluff—an experience never very far away from the streets—he nevertheless thought that he had never met anyone who could be compared with her—except perhaps—perhaps—: a few cinematographic apparitions. And anyway, there was something of that about her: the blondness of her hair, the hollowness of her cheeks, the contours of her hips. That would be a compliment to pay her. Pierrot shut his eyes, conjured up the hubbub of the dodgem cars, the aerodynamism of the little vehicle in which he had pressed up against her; and then he once again felt the effects of the disturbing perfumes in which she had drenched herself, once again he felt queasy at the mnemonic olfaction of this sexual allure, and for a few moments he lost himself in the revivescence of the odors that gave such luxurious attraction to feminine sweat.

He thought he was going to faint.

He reopened his eyes. The Seine was still flowing, still as beautiful, still as phlegmy. The motionless straw hats were keeping watch on their sterile lines. A dog, a bastard mongrel, was merrily rolling in some excrement. On the Argenteuil bridge and the main road, cars and trucks were still circulating.

Pierrot breathed in a great basinful of air. He was still quite agitated. Decidedly, this was the real thing, the great romance, true love. He lights another cigarette from the dying stub of the previous one which he had put down by his side, and reconsiders the situation in great earnest. That he'd got it badly, he could not doubt. All he had to think of now, then, was its realization and, in the first place, a further meeting. He began to chew over all this as on a tender blade of grass, though without managing to arrive at a positive, practical plan of action. Towards the end of the afternoon he stood up, completely benumbed, and stretched. He had not devised any scheme worth retaining, unless it was to go back to the Rue des Larmes the next day at around eleven, but he was pleased to know that he was in love, and he went back to Paris vaguely whistling a tune he didn't know but in which, if he had been more of a musician, he would have been able to recognize the one that had been exuded by the pick-up of the bumper car track while he was therein conveying, far-removed from the impacts, the lovely bird he had just flushed, and by whom he was now so smitten.

He reached the Uni Bar quite some time before he was due to report to Crouïa Bey. He goes in and finds Petit-Pouce and Paradis there, each with a plate of sauerkraut in front of him, and a beautiful half of light ale. They'd won on the pari-mutuel.

"Well, my old buddy," said Paradis, "you coming to sit with us?"

"Yes," said Pierrot.

"What'll it be for Monsieur?" asked the waitress (a terrific hustler, this one).

"A bock and a ham sandwich with mustard," said Pierrot.

"Bring him a sauerkraut and a half," said Paradis to Fifine (the terrific hustler). "It's on me."

"You got yourself thrown out again last night, so it seems?" inquired Petit-Pouce, busily absorbed in the absorption of a big cylinder of sausage.

"Yes," Pierrot replied, laughing, "but that's not going to stop me returning today."

"No?" said Petit-Pouce.

"How're you going to go about it, pal?" asked Paradis.

Pierrot explained his new profession.

"Good god," said Paradis ecstatically, "can you imagine?"

Fifine brought the sauerkraut, and while Pierrot fell to with enthusiasm, the other two resumed their erudite, and documented, discussion on the merits of the little gee-gees capable of getting terrific odds and providing further blow-outs.

Pierrot caught them up with the dessert, and Paradis ordered three cafés-cognacs.

"So," said Petit-Pouce to Pierrot, "you chat up the superboss's daughter?"

"Me?" said Pierrot. "Well, I talk to her."

"Come to that, you'd be making a big mistake if you didn't try," said Petit-Pouce, "there's some that have made it before you."

"You're not among them," said Paradis.

"And anyway, what's it matter?" said Pierrot, wiping his glasses with a bit of the tissue-paper tablecloth.

He smiled complacently.

Petit-Pouce thought he had a face that was just asking to be slapped.

"Shall we measure our skill?" he proposed, jerking his shoulder in the direction of a pin-table.

"Not this evening," said Paradis. "We haven't got time."

"I'll come with you," said Pierrot, putting his glasses on again. "I've got to be there at eight."

At the Uni Park gate, no one made any objection to his entering. One of the muscle-men who happened to be there pretended not to see him. Petit-Pouce and Paradis left Pierrot, who made his way to the first booth on the right, where bills and streamers announced the arrival of Crouïa Bey and described his exploits with the customary acclamations. There were pictures showing the personage with hooks inserted under his shoulder blades and towing a Rolls Royce, or swallowing a mixture of bits of broken bottle and red-hot spikes. Pierrot made a face; he found this repugnant.

He went in by the back door. Crouïa Bey was already there in full array, preparing his act.

"You're none too early," he said. "Get inside this uniform, there, yes, that's right, well, step on it, stir your stumps, get the lead out of your arse, or ass if you prefer, that's it at last, come here now and let me black your face, take your specs off then, dope, that's it, and let me polish your mug, there, that's okay now, put your turban on, there, well, you look fine, that'll do."

Then he explained in detail what he had to do.

The barker came to inquire whether he could get going. They were ready to start. So he activated the pick-up and it began to spew out "Travadja the Temptress" and Ravel's "Bolero" and, when some lechers, presuming that there was going to be a belly dance, had stopped in front of the establishment, he began to spout his patter. Pierrot stood stock-still, in Persian costume.

At last the house filled and the curtain rose on a whole collection of ironmongery. Pierrot was there too, no less rigid than before. When the fakir made his entrance, he crossed his arms over his chest and bowed very low. Hm, I managed that salute pretty well, he thought. The fakir gave him a signal. Pierrot, with an infinitely submissive gesture, presented him with a hatpin fifty centimeters long which Crouïa Bey stuck in his right cheek. Its point came out through his mouth. On a further signal, Pierrot handed him another pin which proceeded to perforate his other cheek. A third pin once again transpierced his right cheek, and so on.

Absorbed in his work, Pierrot at first paid very little attention to what had become of the first hatpins. But before presenting the sixth, he raised his eyes. Through a fog, he caught sight of things that looked like steel spikes emerging from the fakir's beautiful beard. He blanched. His eyes followed the shaft of the latest pin: it rose up into the air, and then slowly, having pierced the skin, penetrated the flesh. With staring eyes, Pierrot looked at this, pale with horror. Then the point reappeared between the two lips. Pierrot could hold out no longer. Pierrot fainted.

The audience laughed like anything.

4

IN THE TREE UNDER HER WINDOW, the little sparrows were chirruping. In the street, the cars were hooting. The roar of all the traffic came hurtling in through the wide-open window. It must already be quite late. Suddenly, the quarreling sparrows flew off in a flock, straight up into the sky. Yvonne, who was opening her eyes, saw them go by.

She remained motionless for a few moments, in the same position she had slept in, curled up like a gundog. Only her gaze was active. A big pigeon hovering in the distance could not escape it. Then, having ended their quarrel, the neighboring birds came down again into their tree, where they once more began to twitter madly. The blue rectangle of the sky thus only allowed itself to be sullied by passing, sometimes almost imperceptible flights. Yvonne liked her landscapeless window, which didn't impose anything on her. She had grown up in front of it: she was twelve when she slept in this room for the first time; she was nineteen now.

Some time took place. An alarm clock demonstrated this assiduously, by the measured course of its hands—a silent alarm clock, and, at night, luminous, an improved model.

Yvonne, who was facing it, looked at it, examined it, and then began to do some rapid mental arithmetic. Having resolved the problem (her timetable for the morning), she turned over on to her back and began to stretch. She felt all her muscles wake up and shake themselves like a pack of young hounds, lively and skittish. Then she unbuttoned her pajama jacket and caressed her chest, while applying herself to the control of her breathing, following the advice of the best fashion magazines. Decidedly, it was time for physical culture.

With a sweeping, cinematographic gesture, she threw back her covers, jumped out of bed and, lying down on a rug ad hoc, began the few movements that give women a flat stomach, small, arrogant breasts, a slender waist, streamlined thighs and a nice firm posterior. This lasted for a good twenty minutes; she was applying herself to such effect that she couldn't think of anything else, and the strange poses she adopted did not give rise in her to any of the evil thoughts they would have inspired in a male spectator. Moreover, these were not the only attentions her body demanded; without mentioning the accomplishment of her natural functions, which in her case occurred with the same regularity and perfection as her purely feminine rhythm, Yvonne had to rub down this body, bathe it, douse it, perfume it, give it the best possible appearance, it, as well as its complements: nails, hair, eyebrows. It had to be nourished, with great appetite. It had to be clothed, which required choice and precision. It had to be looked at, in mirrors.

It was only when she had to wait for a varnish at the end of her fingers to dry, a varnish more blackish than blood-red, that Yvonne had a little time to think of another being than herself. And straightaway it was young Perdrix who came to the fore. Huh! she'd had enough of *him!* He didn't even give her any pleasure. And so stupid; no imagination. Good-looking, but he made a lousy lover, almost a cretin. And it had already lasted three days. Three wasted days. She'd been decent to him long enough, she could give him the push now. She saw herself again, with him in the boat on the Magic River—and how scared she'd been that they were going to capsize with the craft. It was laughable; and she laughed. When she'd finished laughing, and as the varnish was still not dry, she returned to the person of young Perdrix: insipid. She, Yvonne, had no taste for him, that person. Of all the lovers she'd tried, he was certainly the least amusing: unforgivable. And then, there was no poetry about the fellow: no, this was still not true love. Ah! true love, it comes, you don't know when, you don't know how, and, furthermore, you don't know who for. At least, that's how it seems. And then it's nothing but moonlit nights, gondolas, ethereal raptures, soulmates and sweet innocence. Comic.

Yvonne deemed it pointless to consider this mystery at any greater length and decided, in any case, to give young Perdrix the brush-off that very evening. He would turn up, with a smug smile, expecting his pleasure, and she would say "hands off, young man," he would be amazed, et cetera; in short, it wouldn't present any difficulty. And anyway, the varnish was dry: en route. She made a few slight alterations to her toilette, placed a hat on her head, and then, with a glance over her shoulder, made sure that the seam of her stockings was rising quite perpendicularly up her legs. Then she went out of her room and down the stairs, fresh and light as a summer springtime.

She passed the concierge's lodge, and that person called out "good morning, Mademoiselle Yvonne," while thinking in the inside of her innermost heart, "Just look at her, that's no respectable girl." She could have said these things to her out loud, they wouldn't have surprised Yvonne, who was far from unaware of all that was thought about her in the house, and they wouldn't have upset her either, because what did she care, huh, what the hell did it matter? When she got to the door she came to a sudden halt, it was as if she had collided with the wall of light that rose up in front of her. She arranged those details of her toilette that had been able to wait until this instant when a woman is going to become for the men in the street the abstract epitome of their desires.

She remained motionless for a few moments, absorbed in the joy of herself and the joy of the life shining before her.

She was just about to take her first step when she realized that the kind of alternating murmur she could hear, mingled with the normal sounds of the avenue towards eleven in the morning, was coming from one of the ground floor rooms, whose window was open and shutters closed. She only had to move very slightly forward to catch the words spoken in an undertone that composed this sordino. These low voices were two, and in one of them Yvonne recognized that of Léonie. She was saying:

"I can't help wondering why you didn't want to tell me who you are."

The other voice said—and it could only be that of Crouïa Bey, who Yvonne knew was occupying this room, but whose accent she had difficulty in recognizing:

"I didn't know you'd known my brother."

"I recognized you right away."

"I find that extraordinary."

"That's the way it is, Sidi Mouilleminche. I'm a physiognomist."

"Phenomenal."

"But why didn't you tell me at once that you were his brother?"

"I have a role to play, don't forget, Madame."

"That's true. Was that the only reason?"

"No doubt."

"So he's dead?"

"I told you he was."

"And he died just like you told me?"

"Just like I told you."

"In his letters, didn't he ever say anything about me?"

"He was very discreet about his affairs of the heart."

"One day, he suddenly disappeared. That was twenty years ago."

"Yes."

"I looked everywhere for him. I was crazy. My first love!"

"I understand."

"I've never heard any talk of him since."

"He'd changed his stage name. He was called Torricelli, then."

"Did he go on tours?"

"Yes. I was traveling, too. I didn't get much news of him."

"And it happened in Palinsac?"

"Yes."

"And the girl, who was she?"

"He had known others between you and her, permit me to tell you."

"That's not the point. The woman for whom, because of whom, he died, who is she, where is she?"

"How can you go on thinking about those old stories? The only thing to do with the past is forget it, believe me."

"That's your opinion. It isn't mine."

"You're wrong, believe me."

"I loved him."

"Well then, forgive me for having revived such painful memories in you."

"Thank you for having talked to me about him. Very genuinely: thank you. Adieu, Sidi Mouilleminche."

Yvonne heard Léonie opening the door of the room. She walked off.

She found it hard to imagine what she might be in twenty years, and even harder to imagine herself thinking of—for example—Perdrix junior, who, it's true, wasn't the first. What particularly struck her about the dialogue she had just overheard was the designation of "Sidi Mouilleminche" by which Léonie had addressed Crouïa Bey, which implied some intimacy, which seemed unlikely; it could only, therefore, be the latest proof of the eccentricity of that person. And the next thing that struck Yvonne was the precision and intensity of the memory that bound Léonie to her first lover, an intensity and precision that seemed as absurd as the way people behave in dreams. She certainly must have had it badly if she was still so worked up about it! Funny sort of woman! Comic!

Yvonne crossed the Rue des Larmes, making her way to the Rue du Pont, and, a few steps farther on, a young man came up and started walking by her side. He'd been running. Yvonne, who'd been accosted more than once, looked him straight in the face and recognized in him a young man who, for several days now, had been chatting her up at her stand in Uni Park. Once, even, he had stood her a ride on the bumper cars, a ride that had ended in a funny sort of way.

What's he going to say?

"I saw you from a distance. I was going for a walk in the Rue des Larmes. I was more or less waiting for you, as you told me."

"Who? Me?"

"You told me you sometimes passed this way, in the mornings."

"You amaze me."

"Oh but you did, I assure you, that's what you told me. Do you mind if I walk a little way with you?"

"You look quite determined to."

"With your permission. With your permission. By the way, do you know what happened to me again yesterday?"

"Why? Do extraordinary things usually happen to you?"

"I don't know whether they're extraordinary, but in any case they aren't ordinary. Didn't your father tell you about it?"

"No."

"Well then, he'd been pretty decent, after what I did to him, do you remember?"

"Ah! that's true."

"Letting me have the job of assistant to the fakir, the new attraction, on the right after the main entrance. And believe it or not, on stage, I was so shaken at the sight of him sticking hatpins into his cheeks that I fainted. He wasn't a bit pleased, the fakir wasn't. Which means that I'm out of a job again."

"Don't expect me to find you one."

"That's the last thing I'd ask! As witness: I've got by up till now. No, I told you that just for something to say. And also to let you know that it wouldn't be very wise for me to show up at Uni Park again. You saw how I was removed the other day?"

"No."

"Your name *is* Yvonne, isn't it?"

"Hm, who told you that?"

"My pals. Do you know that you are the prettiest, the most beautiful, the most gorgeous girl I've ever dared talk to?"

"Is this the presumption that comes with age?"

"I don't think so. It's not my fault, it's yours. When I look at you, I think I'm in the movies. You look as if you've come down from the screen. It's impressive, I assure you."

"And who's your favorite film star?"

"You."

"Ha! And what films have you seen me in?"

"In films just for me, in my dreams. No kidding."

"That's a fine tale!"

"I swear it. Naturally, though, it's much more interesting to be with you in reality."

"For me too: I can hit back. How do I know what you do to me in your dreams? An oddball like you . . . But tell me, does the fakir really stick pins into himself?"

"And how: I got a hell of a shock."

"Then he's a real fakir?"

"Probably, seeing that a fakir is a chap who does things like that. Haven't you been to see him?"

"I can't leave my stand."

"That's true. Incidentally, we had fun the other day in those little cars. Didn't we?"

"Yes. Sort of."

"Couldn't I take you out again one of these days? Not in Uni Park, but somewhere else. We could go to the movies, or dancing."

"The thing is, I'm not free in the evenings at the moment. For the whole season."

"Couldn't you get a girlfriend to replace you just for once?"

"You must be joking. What about my father? He'd go spare."

"Then you're never free!"

"That's what I'm sick and tired of telling you."

"But one morning, early? It's nice going for a walk then; what's more, it's hygienic."

"Thanks; I like to get up late."

She came to an abrupt halt.

"You'll have to leave me, here. I'm going to see someone in this street. See you. I sometimes come this way."

She held out her hand, which he kept in his.

"Then there's no way we can see each other for a bit longer, one of these days?"

"No."

She took back her hand and walked off. Pierrot watched her as she went. A bit farther on she went into a little general store; gathering dust in its window were sticks of licorice, ceramic figures sitting on chamber pots, spools of thread, and illustrated publications, both Gallic and juvenile. Crippled tin soldiers threatened one another with their sabers or their buckled rifles, while authentic old Épinal prints were yellowing to the point of turning russet. Outside the shop, clothes pegs offered the day's papers to the passersby. The shopkeeper usually sat in her back room, and she came running at the sound of the carillon hanging behind the door.

She therefore came darting in when her daughter entered.

"B'jour, M'man," said Yvonne, lightly brushing her lips against the lady's forehead, so as not to leave any lipstick on it.

"Well," said Madame Pradonet joyfully, "so here you are! It's been at least three months since you did me the honor of coming to see me. If I understood your note rightly, you're going to stay and have lunch with me?"

"Yes, M'man," said Yvonne, who'd begun to leaf through a cinematographic gazette.

"What made you decide to come?"

"Nothing," replied Yvonne.

She raised her eyes and offered her mother a gaze about whose candor there could be no discussion.

"Absolutely nothing," she added, and began to look at the pictures again.

"You never were much of a liar," said Madame Pradonet. "How's Eusèbe?"

"Fine."

"And old Léonie?"

"She's got some secrets with the fakir."

Madame Pradonet burst out laughing:

"The fakir? What fakir?"

"I'll tell you later."

"And you, Vovonne, I was forgetting to ask you. Doing all right?"

"Magnificently."

She had finished her magazine. She put it back on the pile of its counterparts.

"We going to have lunch?" she asked.

"Right away, if you like. I'll grill you a steak. Are you still watching your figure?"

The table was laid in the back room. Something was simmering in a saucepan on the gas stove. The two women began to munch some radishes. Madame Pradonet related some vague things about her daily life, the landlord who was discourteous, the cat which was lily-livered, the juvenile clientele who were given to mystification and pilfering; in short, all the little irritations of a tranquil life. And anyway, Madame Pradonet, a small, rather ill-groomed person, spoke of them without conviction, and certainly did not expect her daughter to be interested in them. She was chatting for the sake of chatting, in the first place, and to fill the gaps, in the second place, because Yvonne didn't yet seem inclined to tell her about the fakir. While chatting, she cut herself thick slices of bread and washed them down with white wine. Yvonne noticed that despite her smaller dimensions, her mother's appetite was more or less on a par with Léonie's. Which surprised her.

"What are you looking at like that? her mother asked.

"You certainly can shovel it down," replied Yvonne.

"Well, what d'you expect, at my age there aren't many pleasures left. When I was younger, I had others. If you think it's funny, my life. Ah! your father's a right bastard. Setting that woman up in my home, and then chucking me out as if I was something to be ashamed of."

"You've told me that a hundred times. You shouldn't have let him get away with it: there's revolvers, vitriol, court cases."

Madame Pradonet shrugged her shoulders.

"That's not my style," she said. "But Pradonet will pay for it one day, one way or another, and you know, Vovonne, I shan't even gloat over it. As for Léonie . . . that creature . . ."

"Ah, that's true, I must tell you about the business with the fakir."

"Hold on. I'll do your steak."

While her mother was cooking, Yvonne dreamily disposed her radish stalks in a circle around her plate. Madame Pradonet, who considered herself a psychologist, asked her:

"Are you in love?"

"Me? Huh! Well!"

"Why should that be so surprising? It's happened to other people. Even me, if I didn't still have such strong feelings for your father . . ."

She solemnly raised the fork that had pierced the steak up into the air.

"I sometimes have the impression that it could still happen to me."

"You make me laugh," said Yvonne in a neutral tone of voice.

They got stuck into the meat, which was nicely scorched on the outside and bleeding inside.

"What about that fakir?" asked Madame Pradonet.

"He's called Crouïa Bey. At the moment he's working in the first joint on the right after the main entrance. Not particularly likeable, a beard, round about forty, dark complexion, magnetic eye."

"I can just see him," said Madame Pradonet. "I've known heaps of them like that. Have to be on your guard with them."

"Well," said Yvonne, "believe it or not, when I came out, on my way to see you, I overheard a conversation between Léonie and him."

"Aha! let's hear it."

"I couldn't repeat it exactly, but roughly speaking it was about a chap Léonie was in love with about twenty years ago, who jilted her and who's died since then. And who Crouïa Bey knew."

"You say about twenty years?"

"That's what I thought."

Madame Pradonet did a little mental arithmetic.

"In those days, Léonie and I were great friends. We danced the cakewalk together at the Boite á Dix Sous near the République. We were young, she was younger than me, and we wore short, sequinned dresses above the knee, with black stockings, so we weren't short of admirers. But we kept them at arm's length. We weren't sluts. We knew how to choose. I wonder which one it could be."

"I don't know. But the funniest thing, I thought, was that she called Crouïa Bey 'Sidi Mouilleminche.'"

"Mouilleminche!" exclaimed Madame Pradonet. "How stupid of me not to have thought of him right away. Mouilleminche! But of course! She was completely crazy about him, and that's what she almost became, completely crazy, when he jilted her. He was a good-looking boy and he had a splendid voice. He used to sing at the Boite á Dix Sous, a tenor he was, and the way he used to sing love songs, it was enough to churn up your guts. All the girls used to chase him, not me, but it was Léonie he chose. I said 'not me' because artistes, I never thought they were reliable. I made a big mistake, in the sense that non-artistes can equally well be unreliable, your father for example."

"Poor Papa," said Yvonne. "He thinks he's a great businessman."

"There's no denying, though, that he started out from nothing, and now he's the director of Uni Park. You'll have a fine dowry and a fine inheritance."

"Yes," said Yvonne, with total lack of interest, "but without Léonie he'd never have got there."

Madame Pradonet remained silent. She put the cheese on the table, and some fruit.

"Admit it," said Yvonne.

With the tip of her knife, Madame Pradonet commixed some butter and some Roquefort.

"Admit it," said Yvonne.

"It's possible."

"That's the way it is. You know it better than I do."

"Even so, I'm not exactly the obvious person to sing the praises of Madame Léonie Prouillot!" exclaimed Madame Pradonet.

"No, of course not. Poor Maman."

They said no more and finished their meal in silence. With her coffee, Madame Pradonet always had a small liqueur. Yvonne didn't like liqueurs. She lit an English cigarette.

"She recognized this Crouïa Bey," she went on, in a voice that was indifferent to the tenor of the remarks it was conveying. "I don't know where she'd seen him before. He's the brother of that Mouilleminche."

"I don't know whether he had a brother."

"Are you interested in what I'm telling you? Because personally, you know . . ."

"What else did you hear?"

"Yes. What intrigues Léonie is the girl he died for, this Mouilleminche."

"How was that?"

"Yes. This Mouilleminche died, so it seems, because of some girl in Palinsac, and Léonie wonders who on earth she could be. And mind you, all this was a good ten years ago, if I'm not mistaken. I got the impression that she was more interested in her than in anything else, in that girl. Comic."

"Léonie, you know, in spite of seeming to be such a businesswoman, has always had peculiar ideas from time to time. If it was only having taken Pradonet for her lover. But apart from that, I understand her. When *you* have a past, Vovonne, you'll realize what an odd thing it is. In the first place, there's whole chunks of it that have caved in: absolutely nothing left. Elsewhere, there's weeds that've grown haphazard, and you can't recognize anything there either. And then there's places that you think are so beautiful that you give them a fresh coat of paint every year, sometimes in one color, sometimes in another, and they end up not looking in the least like what they were. Not counting the things we thought very simple and unmysterious when they happened, but which years later we discover aren't so obvious, like sometimes you pass a thing every day and don't notice it and then all of a sudden you see it. That Léonie should be interested in the woman that a man who'd loved her died for, that's only natural. Thoughts like that, and even much more peculiar ones, sprout up in everyone's skull every day, you'll know that when you've had my experience."

"Not very cheerful, all the things you're telling me, M'man."

"And what about you, my girl, tell me a bit about what's been going through your head recently."

"Nothing peculiar, believe me. And even, to be quite accurate, nothing at all."

"Still not thinking of getting married?"

"Oh no!"

"Any admirers?"

"Pah!"

"I know how it is. You must get plenty of propositions at Uni Park. Ah well, that way you get to know men: smart alecks, not one in ten of them would make a halfway decent lover."

"You've got to be right there, I think."

"You'll learn that the proverb 'There are as good fish in the sea as ever came out of it' doesn't apply to decent men. If you lose one, you haven't much chance of digging up another. You don't win the jackpot twice. That's why I, after Pradonet—not to mention the strong feelings I still have for him—I'm not looking. I could if I wanted to, though. But then what? Share my income and my bed with a washed-up old codger and then later on have to nurse his prostate? Thanks a lot! I prefer to remain faithful."

Yvonne listened to this discourse without showing signs of any great emotion. Madame Pradonet went on:

"But you? You haven't said anything. You don't confide in me anymore. Come on, tell me *something* about yourself. I'm your mother, for god's sake!"

Yvonne wondered whether a tiny little glass of liqueur was enough to make a polite person swear. On what did people's dignity depend? . . .

But Madame Pradonet was not drunk; she expressed her

feelings forcefully and invoked the deity just as a lyric poet does.

"God dammit!" she continued, "you come to see me once in three months and you can't find a blind thing to say about yourself."

The carillon by the shop door rang. Madame Pradonet hurried in. Yvonne followed her; she was finishing her cigarette.

Two urchins had come into the shop, all slyness and hypocrisy. Three or four others had their noses glued to the window. Madame Pradonet asked:

"Well, boys, what can I get you?"

One of the two snotnoses pulled a tin soldier out of his pocket and asked:

"You wouldn't have a cap for him would you, M'dame? You see, M'dame, he's Dutch."

"A cap!" said Madame Pradonet in astonishment. "A tin soldier! Of course I wouldn't have one!"

"But M'dame, you can see he hasn't got any rubbers."

The other kid had gone into ecstasies over his colleague's witticisms and was splitting his sides. Moreover, he took advantage of these events to tuck a copy of "Toto-Bonne-Bille" into his jacket, this being a children's comic that was enormously prized by the most waggish representatives of that social category.

Yvonne intervened. "Get out of here, you dirty little beasts," she cried.

The dirty little beasts beat a retreat and barged their way towards the door. The purloined copy of "Toto-Bonne-Bille" resumed its place.

"But Mamz'elle," sniveled the bolder of the two, "we didn't say anything wrong."

"Go on, scram," Yvonne shouted.

She grabbed them by their arms and shook them all the way out to the pavement, to the great and unmerciful joy of their comrades awaiting the outcome of the jape. Yvonne shut the door. They had fled.

"Kids can be so stupid," Madame Pradonet sighed.

"People do the best they can," said Yvonne. "Well then, M'man, thanks for my good lunch, glad you're well, and see you soon."

She kissed her.

"Good bye, my Vovonne," said Madame Pradonet, "and don't leave it too long till next time."

The carillon rang, and Yvonne found herself in the Rue du Pont, so named because it leads to the former Argenteuil bridge, now demolished. The sun was giving all it had, there weren't many people about.

Yvonne walked down this Rue du Pont in the direction of the Avenue de la Porte d'Argenteuil, which she reached shortly afterwards, for barely two hundred meters separated her mother's shop from the conjunction of these two thoroughfares. And then, a stone flying through space passed in front of her nose; this stone had been propelled with great force. Yvonne stopped. She looked around her. Two or three stones came rolling at her feet, creating little clouds on the ground. The young jokers were zealously taking their revenge for their expulsion; they occupied a very strong strategic position, in ambush behind the trees, close to a pile of ammunition waiting to be used for the repair of the highway.

The pranksters began to improve their aim, and the projectiles became less and less approximative. When she was a kid, Yvonne had fought just as much as the boys, and often with them; she knew how it was, so she quite unashamedly ran and took shelter behind a big plane tree. Taking advantage of this first success, her assailants tried a lateral attack; part of their strength crossed the avenue and advanced from tree to tree, operating cross fire. Yvonne retreated from plane tree to plane tree; she was patiently waiting for a courageous passerby to come and disperse the gang of little bastards. She had had sufficient experience of life to know that he couldn't fail to appear and that the number of chances that this would be the case was so considerable that on the human scale this probability became a certainty.

And he did indeed appear. He attacked the main body of the juvenile forces from behind, and dispersed it. He distributed a generous allocation of slaps on the face and kicks on the behind. There was a hasty retreat. The justiciary grabbed hold of the scruff of the neck of the one he imagined to be the ringleader and banged his head several times against a tree trunk, to teach him. Then he sent him flying; the kid grazed his knees on the asphalt, and then scrammed.

The guy went up to Yvonne; she recognized him. He was one of the Uni Park employees on his leisurely way to work. He didn't seem particularly fazed by his battle with the brats; and anyway, this big blond fellow remained calm in most situations, even though "fate" (fatalitas) had so willed it that, in spite of his habitual benevolence towards human beings, he had several convictions for assault and battery.

Paradis raised the anterior part of his headgear a few millimeters and, feigning surprise, exclaimed;

"Goodness! Mademoiselle Yvonne!"

He added, with an interested air:

"Was it you they had it in for, those brats?"

He terminated his preamble with this amused interrogation:

"What on earth could you have done to them?"

"I'd pulled their ears. But it isn't of the slightest importance."

Paradis realized that a few heraldic remarks about children in general and the guttersnipes of the Porte d'Argenteuil in particular would have been greeted with indifference and even rudeness, and that Yvonne wished to change the subject. He therefore found this to say:

"Are you on your way to Uni now. Mademoiselle Yvonne?"

"Yes."

"Do you mind if I come with you?"

"No."

They walked for a time in silence.

Paradis was searching for something to say to her. He found plenty of phrases such as "Well now, a glamour puss like you, I wouldn't mind seeing what's under your dress," or again "Old Pradonet, your penny-pinching papa, when's he going to make up his mind to give us a raise?" but he had a strong feeling that this was not what one should say to Mademoiselle Yvonne and that he must go to the trouble of finding something more uplifting. At first he tried the weather, although he knew, and at the same time as he knew, that that wouldn't lead very far.

"Nice day today," he said.

"Yes," she said.

She looked at him.

She found him attractive. She'd noticed him more than once in Uni Park, but he'd never paid any attention to her.

He, after his attempt at a meteorological conversation, was still wondering what on earth he could come out with, apart from tendentious appreciations of the management of Uni Park or direct invitations to copulation. Of course he had never paid any attention to Yvonne; he knew very well that she was not a quarry for him. Conscious of his social inferiority, he didn't dare raise his eyes to her: he neither wanted to bite off more than he could chew nor risk getting caught up in a tearjerker like you see at the movies or in serials where guys waste away for love of an unattainable dreamboat that at the end you're supposed to believe they marry.

Meanwhile, the proximity of this beautiful girl was beginning to affect him, and, while still searching for his inoffensive subject of conversation, he was trying to think up some honeyed phrases.

But as it was beyond his capacities to think of two things at once, the effort caused him a certain agitation and he didn't dare open his mouth in case he started stammering.

But Yvonne asked him:

"Are you still at the Palace of Fun?"

Ah! There's plenty to chat about there.

"Yes, I still am," he replied.

"Is the work hard?"

"Saturdays and Sundays, and holidays, it's backbreaking, but the other days it's a fairly soft option, so much so that we sometimes go and help our pals out with the merry-go-rounds."

"What do you do there, you personally?"

"Well, I . . ."

But Paradis hesitated. All of a sudden he realized, or thought he realized, that it was rather difficult to explain without hinting at things that ran counter to decency and, as at this very moment he was imagining himself subjecting the boss's daughter, this very girl now walking by his side, to the erotic humiliation he nightly inflicted on all the women who ventured into the Palace, he had some difficulty in finding an answer devoid of precise, concrete implications.

"Oh, you know, there's contraptions, booby traps. I help the ladies over the difficult bits."

"I've never set foot in your Palace," said Yvonne.

This remark immediately transformed Yvonne in Paradis's mind.

All the gossip he'd heard about her vanished, and she

appeared radiant with purity, chastity, virginity.

"But," she went on, "I don't suppose it's a particularly unpleasant job."

The gossip immediately took on new consistency, like black, lowering clouds conjured up by a sorcerer. Paradis decided that Yvonne was perverse, and there and then made up his mind that she would be his, and no later than this selfsame day.

"No, of course not," he said casually, "but it's especially the spectators who get the benefit of it"

"I know," said Yvonne.

This remark took him aback, but even so, he plunged headlong:

"There's a gust of wind that blows the ladies' skirts up, and even the girls' skirts" (he was rather pleased with this "and even the girls' skirts"). "And then, you see, there's a whole load of satyrs, that's the proper word, who come on purpose to get an eyeful. We call them the 'philosophers.' They're depraved."

"What about you?" asked Yvonne, laughing, "doesn't it interest *you*?"

"I'm not saying," he said very rapidly, "but well, spending your whole time doing that, you have to be sick or a bit touched."

"You like more substantial pleasures?"

Paradis, highly embarrassed, wondered what he could possibly find to answer this time. If she made the running, then he'd no longer have the merit of having "seduced" her. And as this was what he intended to do, and moreover what he wished to boast about, he felt somewhat enraged at seeing himself thus forestalled.

"Like everyone else, huh," he said, not looking for any subtleties.

"What do you know about it?" asked Yvonne.

He gave her a sidelong glance. She was taking the piss, it was too much.

"What do I know about it? about what? What other people like, or what *I* like?"

He looked furious, which made Yvonne laugh.

"In short," she concluded, "you don't think much of them, those philosophers."

"Pah!" he said, suddenly very weary, "I don't know. I earn my living, don't I? Some people do worse things."

"I'm not blaming you," said Yvonne.

The moment they got off the subject of the Palace of Fun, Paradis felt better. Out of the corner of his eye, he admired Yvonne. What a glamour puss! And he didn't seem to disgust her. Even though he still wasn't too sure that she wasn't making a sucker of him.

They had crossed the Rue des Larmes and were walking along the walls of Uni Park. They were nearing Pradonet's block.

"Shall we go on walking for another five minutes?" Paradis suggested.

Yvonne looked him straight in the eyes.

"Okay," she said. "Five minutes."

5

MOUNNEZERGUES WAS COOKING his dinner when the bell rang. He was sautéing some potatoes. He turned the gas down under the pan. He wasn't expecting anyone. He imagined for a moment, very romantically, that it was the young man who had taken an interest in the chapel who had come back to see him, to hear more stories, or even out of simple friendship. He opened the door and saw Pradonet.

He showed him into the dining room where his place was already laid, and went and fetched a bottle of aperitif and two glasses. They drank.

"It's a good long time since you came to torment me," said Mounnezergues. "What's new?"

"Nothing," said Pradonet.

"Well then?"

Pradonet drank again.

"The other day, I was on my terrace, showing Uni Park to a visitor. Naturally, he noticed the black patch your chapel makes. Come on, Mounnezergues, what on earth do you care about the Poldevian princes?"

"Is that all?" Mounnezergues asked.

That was all, no doubt, for Pradonet didn't answer.

"Why?" asked Mounnezergues, "why do you expect me to have changed my mind? I'm not a weathercock."

"But for god's sake," cried Pradonet, "once again, what possible obligation can you be under to the Poldevian princes? You don't get a sou out of them. They've completely disappeared. It wouldn't do anybody any harm if the tomb was demolished and your fellow buried in a cemetery like everybody else."

"Pradonet," said Mounnezergues, "it's nearly ten years now that we've been having the same conversation at regular intervals. It's an old habit that we'd miss if we ever managed to come to an agreement"

"But I want that land. And allow me to tell you, Mounnezergues, that I'd be very happy to do without your conversation."

"And for my part, it's your money that I'm happy to do without," said Mounnezergues. "As you well know."

They emptied their glasses.

"A little more?" asked Mounnezergues.

Pradonet seemed to acquiesce. Mounnezergues refilled the two glasses.

"Just because," he went on, "an impolite guest has called your attention to the fact that your land isn't square, that's no reason why I should change my mind. No. Prince Luigi is going to stay buried in that chapel, and I've taken precautionary measures to ensure that after my death things remain that way."

"And what if I had a bomb planted in your chapel, a bomb that would send everything sky high, or if I had your Luigi's remains stolen? What would you say?"

Mounnezergues began to laugh:

"Pradonet," he said, "you never thought up those ideas all by yourself. It was at least Madame Prouillot who put them into your head."

Pradonet sighed.

"You may be sure, Mounnezergues," he said, "that if Madame Prouillot was interested in seeing that bit of land joined on to Uni Park, it would have been done long ago. But she isn't interested. She doesn't think it would give us anything extra."

"She's reasonable," said Mounnezergues.

"Well, *you* aren't," said Pradonet "Refusing a small fortune just to allow an obscure dago to rest in peace!"

"Of course, in peace! Everyone has a right to rest in peace! Do *you* think it's funny, having your skeleton behind glass in a museum, for example? Or again, just think of those Egyptian kings who slept peacefully for centuries until their mummies got carted off to America!"

"You see," cried Pradonet, "one fine day your Prince Luigi, they'll come and dig him up, like the others."

"A simple supposition. And anyway, he'll have had a few years' tranquillity."

"That's enough," said Pradonet, "let's stop this absurd discussion."

He stood up.

"Just a moment!" Mounnezergues exclaimed, "I've something else to say to you. You're always complaining, but I too have cause for dissatisfaction."

Pradonet knew it, but Mounnezergues was determined to mention it yet again.

"Do *you* think it's nice," he demanded, "to have set up an amusement park next to a tomb? Do *you* think that shows respect for the dead?"

"I suppose you'd like me to close down my establishment?"

"I don't know. Think it over."

Pradonet shrugged his shoulders. Mounnezergues stood up and went to the door with his visitor.

"Good evening, Pradonet."

"Good evening, Mounnezergues."

The latter returned to his sautéed potatoes, now almost torrefied. The former slowly made his way towards his house, for it was his dinner time too. Went on his way, then, but not without stopping for a few moments in front of Prince Luigi's modest mausoleum. While gazing at this monument, the strangeness of whose style vaguely worried him, Pradonet was thinking about something completely different. He was thinking—exceptionally—about his wife, but even then he was only thinking about her in a roundabout way, for the course of his cogitations led him in the first place to the defunct personality of Jojo Mouilleminche, Léonie's first lover, and it was only a subsequent reverie that bore him along on its troubled waters until he came up against the image of Eugénie, his legitimate spouse. He arrived home without actually having discovered what was vaguely tormenting him.

During dinner, he observed that Léonie was adopting dreamy attitudes; he also observed that Yvonne was absent.

"What's that bitch up to?"

Yvonne was always on time. She'd been well brought up. Hence this tardiness seemed prodigious. The first idea of the father, as of the false stepmother, was, naturally: dalliance.

"Where the hell can she have been hanging around, the slut?" said Pradonet.

And he is amazed to observe that Léonie wasn't in the slightest bit interested in the imprecations his daughter's vanishing act might inspire in him. Finally, he shut up, and from time to time asked himself vague questions about Crouïa Bey or his brother, the deceased tenor; but he didn't answer them. At nine o'clock, Léonie, returning to her observation post, left him alone in front of his glass of cognac. He went on musing

for a few moments and finally decided in his own mind that
what was bothering him was Crouïa Bey's civil status, because
the fakir had shown him his papers and they didn't at all give
his name as Mouilleminche. So how could he be the brother
of someone called Mouilleminche? Could he have been pulling a fast one on Léonie? Pradonet had thought about this
question subsequently, because the first day, it hadn't struck
him. He thought slowly, but even so he did think, although
he was never very sure of knowing where he was going, and
as, for simple though not easily conjecturable reasons, Crouïa
Bey might have legitimate reasons not to settle for calling himself Mouilleminche, like his brother, he decides not to bother
unduly with this question any more, and he passes on to the
order of the day, which he carries with his own unanimity.
Then he goes up to the terrace.

Things were erupting, as usual, both lights and noises, but
Pradonet's attention was focused only on the zones of silence
and shadow: the Poldevian chapel in the first place, and the
new cause of irritation, the Mamar Circus which had come and
established itself on the other side of the Avenue de Chaillot,
right opposite Uni Park, on a piece of ground on which, some
years before, the desolate remains of an international exhibi-
tion had been dumped. In Léonie's opinion, the presence of
this show wouldn't take any of their customers from them,
but probably bring more. Could be, thought Pradonet, but he
liked to reign alone. His gaze traveled from the tomb to the
tent and from the tent to the tomb, and then, nostalgic and
weary, it came to rest on the dusty, vibrionic agitation which
he prided himself on being responsible for.

Suddenly, this agitation seemed to become organized.
Something like a trough appeared, into which it all collapsed
in waves. From his perch, Pradonet heard a terrific hubbub,

punctuated by shrill cries. Then he saw a little wisp of smoke stretching very gently up to the sky: the philosophers (they were the ones who should be suspected in the first place) were setting fire to the Palace of Fun. Police vans drew up along the pavement near the entrance gate, and Pradonet took a morose pleasure in following the cunning strategy of the patrol's maneuvers in dispersing the demonstrators. Down below, all hell was let loose and there was a full-scale free-for-all. Then came the firemen, who directed their hoses this way and that, drenching everything they thought suspect, conflagrations and rebels alike. The firemen were the first to leave, and they were followed by the constabulary. The merry-go-rounds recommenced their gyrations, and the people hanging around to see the damage were made to move on.

Pradonet then remembered his daughter's absence; he bent over his telescope and looked for the machine-gun range: Yvonne wasn't there. He went down to the dining room, much provoked by so many worries. He had a little drink in passing, and, in no great hurry, continued on his way down. He went out of a little door in his backyard and thus immediately found himself in Uni Park, just behind the chairoplane tower. In front of him, the Palace of Fun was a pathetic sight, scorched and sodden; a mourning letter soaked in tears. Pradonet caught sight of Tortose, who was having an animated discussion with one of his employees. Some cops were moving on the rubbernecks.

"And where d'you think *you're* going?" one of them asked him.

Tortose intervened:

"He's the boss."

To Pradonet, he said:

"Another rotten break! The inspector says that this time it's inevitable, they're going to close down my attraction."

"What happened?" Pradonet asked, very distant, very serene, very Olympian.

Very quietly sad, all things considered.

"Tell the boss what happened," said Tortose to Petit-Pouce.

"I've had my bellyful," said Petit-Pouce.

He had once again been on the receiving end of one or several socks on the jaw, and he was wiping the corner of a peacefully bleeding lip.

"What happened?" Pradonet asked him.

"It was nothing to do with me," said Petit-Pouce, "but that isn't going to stop you giving me the boot."

"We'll transfer you to another attraction," said Pradonet.

"Do you mean it?" asked Petit-Pouce.

"I promise."

Tortose was amazed. But he, in any case, *he* was in dead trouble. Ruined—he will say. What had got into the boss?

"Come on then, tell me!" Pradonet ordered.

"Well, it's like this," said Petit-Pouce. "There's only been two of us since the other day, and that's not enough. Today I was on my own, and that's even less. Paradis, my mate, didn't show up, I don't know what the hell he's doing, maybe he's sick, I don't know, in any case I was on my own, well, that's not enough. There were quite a lot of people, and all the philosophers we usually see, all in their usual places, and their eyes glued to the holes to get a good look at the girls. The thing starts. I get in position to help the birds over the cakewalk. Right. But I couldn't be everywhere. In front of the barrel, no one. The dames didn't want to go through. The ones that had a tough guy with them, he helped them. But then, they didn't stop over the blowhole, did they. 'Course they didn't. And then the philosophers, who didn't see any skirts flying up, they weren't pleased. That's putting it mildly: they hit the roof. Two gorgeous blondes go by right under their noses, and they aren't even allowed to get a squint at anything above the knee. Things are going badly. The buggers are getting worked up. Along comes another girl, and they don't see her panties. They go through the roof. They even start giving me hell. I go down to the barrel. And it's at the cakewalk that things get really rough. I get sworn at. And then the smartest ones decide to take my place. They climb up on to the platform and grab hold of the women, trying to stick them over the blowhole. The gentlemen with these ladies think that the philosophers, well, they're going a bit too far. There's some scuffles. And naturally, it doesn't take long for them to turn into socks on the kisser. Wham! Slam! Bang! Whang! And this is for you, and here's another. The satyrs have gone mad. The women decide to scream their heads off. The wise ones take it on the lam. The obstinate ones try to take advantage of the situation. But the men go on sloshing each other in the chops and jumping on each other's private parts. One dame, I saw this with my own eyes, with her thumb and first finger, she only tries to gouge out the eye of a chap who was starting to grope her. And then just like that, all of a sudden, there's no telling why, no explanations, they all take it into their heads to set fire to the joint. No messing about, it was a marvel how quickly they went to work: a nice little blaze to keep us all happy. After that, the cops arrived: they didn't have any trouble getting the people out, they'd more or less calmed down. And to finish it all off we got the firemen, and they doused the lot."

Petit-Pouce fell silent.

Whereupon Tortose launched into his lamentation:

"And to think that because of those imbeciles, here I am, ruined. The inspector told me so: this makes too many disturbances in quick succession in your establishment, this time we're closing you down for good. And he added that besides, it deserved it, to be closed down, my establishment, and for why? because it was immoral. They took their time noticing it, that that's what it was, immoral, my establishment. And in any case, that's what it is, closed down, my establishment, well and truly closed down, and what's going to become of me, me and my wife and children? Him over there, Petit-Pouce, you're finding him another job, but what about me? Nothing ever changes: the workers always get the breaks. But what about me and my wife and children?"

"You've got some savings, Tortose," said Pradonet.

"Just as well! If I hadn't, there'd be nothing for me to do but croak. But they won't go far."

"You'll invent another attraction, Tortose, I know you."

"No good trying to console me, thanks."

"What more d'you want me to say?"

He held out his hand, which Tortose took flabbily, and then departed. Petit-Pouce reckoned that it was in his interest to stick to the big boss's heels so's not to miss the bus. So he began to walk along by Pradonet's side.

"What show will you put me in, Monsieur?" he asked.

Pradonet turned and looked at him as if he had just discovered him:

"I'll let you know," he said.

"Very well, Monsieur."

No good insisting. Petit-Pouce hadn't reached the age of forty-five without becoming aware of what you have to take in life, the bitter pills you have to swallow, the number of times you have to let people spit in your face and then simply wipe the gob off—and tell them thank you, what's more. He therefore judged it pointless to hang on any longer, and he stayed where he was, like a post.

As people kept bumping into him, he moved on.

He hadn't sufficiently insisted on the fact that none of this would have happened if Paradis hadn't failed to show up without warning, or if Pierrot had been replaced; especially, if Paradis hadn't failed to show up. But he hadn't wanted to do the dirty on Paradis. And anyway, this bad deed wouldn't have been of the slightest use, seeing that his pal would in any case get the boot. Petit-Pouce began to reflect on his life as a whole (his own life), while his eye automatically registered the presence of the philosophers in front of a merry-go-round on which girls showing a lot of thigh were perched on pigs, and the absence of Yvonne from her machine gun. He saw his entire life flashing in front of his eyes, as drowning people are always supposed to do, in pictures with subtitles: parents, primary school, apprenticeship, military service, the A.Z. private detective agency (All Types of Inquiries, Divorce Our Speciality), first dodgy transaction, first swindle, first blackmail, marriage, further dodgy transactions, further swindles, further blackmail, confrontation with the police (the real police), expiation, redemption, the lousy little jobs, the least brilliant of which was certainly not that of assistant torturer at the Palace of Fun. He had done worse. And the wife: not easy; and the kids: as a bonus.

Petit-Pouce touched the bottom of the abyss with his foot and then suddenly came up to the surface again, swept up in a vortex of hatred. Then he saw the philosophers and shrugged his shoulders. Then he saw the deserted stand, and immediately linked Yvonne's absence with that of Paradis. He tried to spot some fellow with whom he could pick a quarrel and exchange a few wallops. He was bursting with resentment, despair, bitterness. He cast ferocious eyes around him, but all they lighted on was Pradonet, accompanied by the person people called Madame Pradonet.

His ideas of getting into a scrap abandoned him abruptly, and his first plan of sticking to the big boss's heels once again seemed excellent So he advanced surreptitiously, but by the time he had caught up with Léonie, Pradonet had disappeared, no doubt continuing on his round. Petit-Pouce stopped short. Léonie photographed him.

She beckoned to him. He thought he had read her signal correctly, and went up to her. He pinched the buttocks of his felt hat, raised it a few millimeters above his head, replaced it on its pedestal, and waited.

"You did work at the Palace?" the lady asked.

"Yes, Madame Pradonet," he replied, with a servile smile.

"Then you're out of a job?"

Hard as hell, the old bag. Petit-Pouce protested, stammering:

"The boss, Monsieur Pradonet, he promised me, they'd take me on in another show . . ."

"Yeah," said Léonie. "Are you sure they will?"

"He promised me. Monsieur Pradonet promised me."

"Wasn't it your fault, that there was a riot?"

"Me? My fault? Oh no, Madame Pradonet. Just think, I was on my own, instead of the three we usually are."

"Where were the others?"

"One was sacked a few days ago and hadn't been replaced and the other didn't come this evening, I don't know why not, he must be ill."

Petit-Pouce then realized that his interlocutrix wasn't the least bit interested in what he was telling her and was amusing herself by making him talk. And indeed, she suddenly asked him:

"You were in the police once?"

"Yes, Madame."

He felt a spasm in the region of his glottis, but he couldn't deny it. And yet . . . He corrected himself:

"That's not entirely accurate, Madame Pradonet. I worked for a private agency."

"You know how to conduct an inquiry."

This, on Léonie's part, was just as affirmative as it was interrogative; more a desire than a doubt.

Petit-Pouce felt reassured. No doubt about it, she wanted to send him in pursuit of her daughter, of her stepdaughter, rather, of Yvonne, that was. And as he knew where she was, for he had no doubt that she had gone gallivanting, and worse, with Paradis, a feeling of jubilation began to bubble up in him, which he had difficulty in containing. Even so, he couldn't help declaring:

"*Have* I conducted inquiries, Madame? I'll say I have. And I've pulled off some particularly sticky ones."

"No need to boast. What I'm going to ask you won't be at all difficult."

"Were you thinking of entrusting me with one?" asked Petit-Pouce, trembling with impatience (all the more so in that he was anticipating a job that was already in the bag).

"Yes, and these are my conditions."

"They will be mine, Madame Pradonet."

"A thousand francs and a steady job here, if you succeed. Thirty francs a day for your cigarettes. A thousand-franc advance for your expenses. More, if need be. You will account for your expenditure. In a week from now, you should have finished. Does that suit you?"

"Yes, Madame Pradonet. Oh yes, Madame Pradonet."

He had the impression that there were flashes of sunlight on the back of his neck. He could have wept.

"And what do I have to do, Madame Pradonet? What do I have to do?"

Léonie pushed him into a shady corner.

It's that, all right, thought Petit-Pouce, it's about the girl that's gone to the bad, they want me to find her.

"I'm listening, Madame Pradonet," he said.

"Well, here's what you have to do: find out the exact circumstances in which, about ten years ago, a person called Jojo Mouilleminche died in Palinsac; and if, as I have been told, he died for love of a girl, find the girl."

"You did say: ten years ago?"

"Yes."

"The thing is, that won't be very easy."

He was slightly furious to see that it was real work.

"It's feasible," said Léonie.

She took some money out of her bag. Petit-Pouce decided that, after all, he was in luck. He accepted it and thanked her.

"Even so, I'll need some more information."

He said that to hide the emotion he felt at the touch of this silky bank note, not out of professional conscience.

"You can get by with that," said Léonie. "And anyway, *I* don't know any more either."

"But what did he do, for instance, this Mouilleminche?"

"He was a singer."

"There. You see, you do know more."

"He sang in cafes-concerts, first under the name of Chaliaqueue and then under that of Torricelli. He must have been about thirty when he died. This time, that really is all."

"And the girl?"

"She would have been his mistress."

"One more fact you had omitted to give me."

"That's enough, Monsieur Petit-Pouce. You needn't start trying to be clever because you've just pocketed a thousand-franc note. Don't forget that you're going to account for all your expenses. Well, I suppose the simplest thing is to go there to conduct your inquiry. There's a train that leaves tomorrow morning at five. Why don't you take it? And you'll report back to me every day. Is that understood?"

"Yes, Madame. I'll leave this very night, Madame Pradonet."

"Good. And you must sign this."

She shows him a paper: a receipt for a thousand francs. Petit-Pouce signs. She puts the paper back in her bag. Having told Petit-Pouce that she hopes she'll soon receive the telegram in which he announces that he has found the girl in question, she departs.

When Léonie had gone, Petit-Pouce wondered whether the girl in question might not quite simply be Pradonet's daughter, and whether he hadn't been addressed in a coded language which he hadn't understood but was supposed to be able to decipher. This thought tormented him for a while and spoilt the pleasure he was anticipating at the idea of going for a little trip with a nicely bulging wallet.

After wandering around Uni Park for a while, casting a listless eye on this or that attraction, he finally convinced himself that the lady's language had been perfectly clear and that he had to set off for Palinsac at crack of dawn. So he'd have to go home first to get a suitcase and take leave of his missus—at the same time being very careful not to let the said person suspect the existence of the thousand-franc note. Reconsidering it, this note, he seemed to become aware of a burning sensation over his chest, in the region of his wallet, and he immediately got the idea of making inroads into the said note. He hurried out of the Park in the direction of the Uni Bar, with the intention of getting down a sauerkraut and several half pints.

As he entered the café, the first two people he saw were Yvonne and Paradis. If only it had been to do with her, he said to himself with some regret, my inquiry'd already be over. Paradis was sitting beside Yvonne and rubbing himself up against her like a rabbit in rut. He didn't seem embarrassed by the presence of Petit-Pouce and made a sign to him that he interpreted as an invitation to sit at their table. Asking himself whether his buddy had already slept with the girl or whether it was for later, he went over.

"Do you recognize him?" Paradis asked Yvonne. "He's the pal who works with me at the Palace."

"Who used to work," said Petit-Pouce, sitting down and projecting his felt hat in the direction of a peg, on which it came to rest.

"Why 'used to work'?" asked Paradis, moderately alarmed.

"What, haven't you heard?" said Petit-Pouce in astonishment, and, acting polite towards Yvonne, he added, "Maybe you'd rather I didn't, but I've got a kind of craving for a sauerkraut . . ."

They were drinking Benedictine.

"That's perfectly all right," said Yvonne. "You can stuff yourself with anything you like, even with . . ."

Paradis put his hand over her mouth.

"She's had a little to drink," he said to Petit-Pouce.

"Have you got the latest edition of *Paris-Soir*?" inquired the latter.

"Yes. But I haven't won anything."

Petit-Pouce looked carefully for his number. They both risked eleven francs on each draw. Sometimes they got their money back. In between times, they made plans; when the lucky break came, it wouldn't catch them napping. But this time, once again, it hadn't come up trumps.

Petit-Pouce gave the paper back to his pal.

"Never mind," he said, getting stuck into his sauerkraut.

"You look as if you're starving," Paradis remarked.

"Not so specially. It's only for the pleasure."

"It stinks," said Yvonne.

"Well, I did warn you. But if it bothers you. I'll go and sit somewhere else."

"She's only trying to get a rise out of you," said Paradis.

He pulled Yvonne up close to him. She shook him off, but without protesting. Petit-Pouce couldn't manage to form an opinion.

"Well then," asked Paradis, who still had some slight misgivings, "did everything go all right without me?"

"And how," replied Petit-Pouce, chewing a bit of sausage.

"Yes? or no?"

"Hang on. I'll tell you."

And he piled up some mustard and sausage on a bit of bread. Yvonne watched him with amused disgust.

"I'm thirsty," she said to Paradis.

"You've had enough," said Paradis.

He was terrified of her getting drunk. He guessed that in that state she'd create a scandal. Which didn't amuse him.

But she called the waiter.

"A half!"

"On top of Benedictine, that makes people sick," said Paradis.

"Me too, another half," said Petit-Pouce, who was methodically finishing his sauerkraut.

"Me too, then," said Paradis, who was now sure of seeing the evening ending in punch-ups and cascades of vomit.

Yvonne was smiling straight ahead of her, already well oiled and enchanted at the idea of drinking beer on top of Benedictine in front of a brawny character who was busy shoveling down sauerkraut, all that in the midst of clouds of smoke, ugh! She went on smiling.

The waiter brought the three halves. There had been a little silence. Petit-Pouce had just dunked up the last drop of juice still stagnating in his plate.

"Right," said he.

And, addressing his mate, jovially:

"Well, believe it or not, they've given me the sack."

"No kidding?" asked Paradis, frowning.

Yvonne turned round to him and laughed in his face:

"But you too, you big booby!" she cried.

"Of course," said Petit-Pouce cordially.

Paradis pulled a long face. He'd taken Yvonne gallivanting all day, he'd invited her to dinner, he'd paid assiduous court to her, backed up by persistent necking, but never for one moment had he imagined that he might be fired. He had confidence in life. He'd had a good day (although not quite totally so, as he hadn't been able to persuade Yvonne to grant him what she had granted young Perdrix (he was sure), young Tortose (this was probable), and Paroudant of the Alpinic Railway (as rumor had it)).

He found something to say:

"Me, I understand, but you?"

He was addressing Petit-Pouce.

The latter stifled a belch between his teeth and uttered several horse laughs that detonated like farts. He was in an excellent mood and, full of brio, related the incidents that had brought about the closure of the Palace of Fun.

"Even so, have to go and see tomorrow, whether it's closed for good," said Paradis.

"I've already told you it is," said Petit-Pouce. "It's irrevocable. What'll you do now?"

He was still looking at the two of them, wondering whether yes or no they had fornicated. This intrigued him enormously, and he even felt kind of sad to think that he was going off to the provinces without having got to the bottom of the matter.

Paradis, for his part, was trying to think up an answer. He guessed that his pal wasn't worried and that he must already have found himself another job. So he didn't want to gladden his heart too much by confessing that he was going to be up the creek. He said:

"Oh, me, you know, I can wait. We went to Vincennes, me and Yvonne, and I backed a winner. So I'm going to take it easy. I feel like doing a bit of camping in the Midi now."

"Good idea," said Petit-Pouce, who didn't believe a word of this tale, but reckoned it was aimed at the bird, not at him.

"He won five thousand," said Yvonne. "So he's going to stand us a bottle of bubbly."

"After the beer!" Paradis groaned.

The waiter who, feeling that morale was a little shaky in that direction, was prowling around the table, hurried up to take the order.

"You're often a lucky bastard," said Petit-Pouce to his pal. "I've seen him win several times," he added, for Yvonne's information, "in cases where he didn't have the slightest chance, with impossible nags. Yes, but, luck of that sort doesn't go with love. Isn't that right?"

"You prat," Paradis murmured.

And, somewhat louder:

"And you, cleverguts, what are you going to do?"

"Me?" said Petit-Pouce, savoring the sweet blandishments of hypocrisy, "me? I'm right up the creek. What's going to become of me? With the wife? and the kids?"

"Poor old chap," said Paradis, now positive that Petit-Pouce had got himself a job somewhere else.

The waiter brought the sparkling wine with a sprightly step and uncorked it magisterially. He poured. They drank.

"To your luck. To your loves," said Petit-Pouce.

"To your next job," said Paradis.

Yvonne emptied her glass and stood up:

"Well," she said, "I'm going now."

She held out her hand to Paradis, and he tried to keep it in his:

"Wouldn't you like me to . . ."

"Oh, you stay with your friend"

He didn't dare insist.

At the door, she met Pierrot, who was coming in.

"Evening," she said in passing.

He hadn't had time to recognize her. He watched her as she went, and then turned his attention to the café, where he saw Petit-Pouce and Paradis. He went over to their table.

"How's things?" he asked cordially.

He then discovered in his head that the young woman he'd just passed was Yvonne. He sat down and saw the three glasses.

"Well well," he said, "was she drinking with you?"

"I spent the day with her," said Paradis, who felt like grinding his teeth and who was rolling his eyes, which were white with fury, alarmingly.

But he considered that Yvonne's departure had made him look ridiculous in Petit-Pouce's eyes.

"Did you or did you not sleep with her?" Petit-Pouce asked him.

"That any of your business?"

"I see; she strung you along."

"Who? me?"

"She must have got through quite a bit of your jack."

"I'm in the habit of paying for the women I go out with. I'm not a pimp."

"Yerra," said Petit-Pouce.

He turned to Pierrot, with the extremely satisfying impression of having flattened a pal and of leaving him prostrate on the floor. The fact is that, having withered him with a look, Paradis had been content to pour himself a glass of wine which he had knocked back in one gulp, as he'd seen actors do in the movies when they have to perform gestures of despair.

"Well then," he said to Pierrot, "did you know that the Palace of Fun has been closed down?"

"No," said Pierrot, with indifference.

"There was a fight. The philosophers had started a fire."

"No kidding," said Pierrot.

He was totally unmoved. All the same, Petit-Pouce asked him:

"And you, what're you doing now?"

He didn't answer immediately. He too was asking himself questions about what might have happened between Yvonne and Paradis, but he was in possession of far fewer points of reference than Petit-Pouce; he was therefore rather inclined to believe that the other two: yes. This only slightly surprised him, although he was somewhat saddened; he would very much have liked to know the means employed by his friend to achieve this result. As he saw the waiter passing, he requested him to bring another glass, so that he too could participate in the consumption of the bottle of sparkling wine.

"You were asked what you were doing now," said Paradis, pouring him a drink.

"Nothing," said Pierrot.

This reply, although inexact, didn't surprise anyone, they were so used to hearing it from all and sundry. Their friend immediately continued:

"Here, you know the little chapel behind the Alpinic Railway?"

"What d'you suppose I care about your chapel?" said Paradis, who was mulling over his rout, and had never yet bothered his head with religious archeology.

Petit-Pouce, who had pretentions, among which were those of being an acute observer and of knowing the district by heart (he was still influenced by his former profession, which he was about to resume, sort of), said:

"The one in the Rue des Larmes?"

"Do you know what it is?"

They could hardly pretend that they did, since he seemed to have the answer off pat. They contented themselves with sinking what was left of the wine, and Petit-Pouce, who was getting into the habit of spending, stood them another bottle, because if he had to catch the five o'clock train there was no point in going to bed.

"You still haven't told us what you're going to do," he said to Pierrot, with increased benevolence.

"Nothing special for the moment. But to come back to the chapel, I won't tell you what it is, since you don't seem to be interested, but . . ."

"Oh but we are," said Paradis, who was beginning to forget Yvonne, the price of the bottle, and his dismissal from the Palace, "oh yes, tell us, we want to learn."

"Can you imagine, I've made the acquaintance of the guardian of the chapel. He's really someone."

"Continue, you interest us," said Petit-Pouce who, being older than the other two, occasionally used out-of-date expressions.

"In the old days, he owned all the land where Uni Park is now, he inherited it from his family, he's a real gent."

"Seeing that you're so clever," said Petit-Pouce, "do you know who all that land belongs to now?"

"Doesn't it belong to Pradonet?" asked Paradis, who didn't despair of becoming the boss's son-in-law.

"To Pradonet!" exclaimed Petit-Pouce. "To that big booby! Not likely. What's more, I'll bet you don't know how Uni Park was founded, or who by."

"What do we care?" said Paradis.

"Tell us just the same," said Pierrot.

Petit-Pouce drank some wine, dried his moustache with the back of his hand, and said:

"Four of them got together, Pradonet first, naturally, it was his idea. He owned a really nice ride, and he had a bit stashed away. Then came Prouillot, his pal. He brought the Alpinic Railway with him, and his wife, who you now know under the name of Madame Pradonet but who's no more Madame Pradonet than I am the Pope . . ."

"How d'you know all this?" Paradis asked.

"Prouillot, he died," Petit-Pouce continued, "and his wife, naturally, everything got left to her. But that's not all."

"And Yvonne," Pierrot asked. "Whose daughter is she?"

"Pradonet's and his first wife's, he ditched her and now she has a little haberdashery in the Rue du Pont."

"I get it," said Pierrot.

"What do you get?" asked Petit-Pouce.

"How d'you know all this?" asked Paradis.

"The third partner," Petit-Pouce went on, "was Perdrix, who you both know; a dimwit. His share wasn't very big, and it's stayed that way. The fourth one's called Pansoult, he's the so-called Madame Pradonet's uncle. He's the one the grounds belong to."

"Ah, I see," said Pierrot "He's the one Mounnezergues sold them to."

"Mounnezergues?"

"Yes, the guardian of the tomb of the Poldevian prince."

"Poldevian?"

And he told them what he knew about the chapel in the Rue des Larmes, about the Poldevians, and about their princes.

The other two listened to him because they liked stories and had become dreamy. Paradis was no longer very sure where he was. Petit-Pouce told himself that it was a good thing to know this prehistory of Uni Park, and thought himself very wise. He was also pleased to see the evening becoming so long-drawn-out because he was hoping not to go to bed before he left for Palinsac at five.

Pierrot exhausted all his knowledge, with the possible

exception of the odd detail, though, which he had forgotten. And then they all three drank, and Petit-Pouce, to take their minds off things, suggested a game of twenty-sous pinball. It so happened that the Uni Bar boasted a splendid machine on which, every time you scored a thousand points, a little naked doll lit up. Pierrot accepted enthusiastically, and Paradis languidly, but the boss objected that it was five to two and he was closing. The match was postponed to some other time and the waiter approached. Petit-Pouce pointed out that one bottle was on him and pulled his wallet out of his hip pocket. But he still didn't show his thousand-franc note. He was waiting to see what Paradis would do. And Paradis did what he had foreseen, and Petit-Pouce admired himself for being so sagacious: he borrowed a hundred francs from him.

Then they went to a crummy little bar to have one last drink. After which Petit-Pouce went home, packed his suitcase and, leaving his wife half-asleep and understanding very little, at five o'clock caught the train to Palinsac.

6

Pierrot was woken at about seven by the hotel maid. She'd just seen it announced in the stop-press in bold type that Uni Park, this very night, had been burned down. This news deeply interested Pierrot, who for a moment feared for Yvonne, but no casualties were announced. The paper ended its report by informing its readers that the cause of the catastrophe was not known but that experts were going to try to solve the problem.

"So now you're out of a job, Monsieur Pierrot," said the maid, who thought he was still employed there.

She looked at him with sympathy and compassion. Only his head was above the sheets; for the rest, he was naked. As he had gone to bed very late, after having drunk slightly more than usual, he had great difficulty in opening both his eyes at the same time.

"I'm afraid so," he replied. "I'll have to go and see what's happening."

But he had no desire to go rushing to the scene of the disaster, and if he said "I'll get up," it was only to persuade the maid to leave the room. This result obtained, he closed his eyes again and went back to sleep for another hour or so. This supplementary ration of sleep he had considered necessary.

His enclothing and his toilet were accompanied only by vague reveries accompanied by the spasmodic humming of well-known refrains. It was only while he was having his coffee at the nearby bistro that he judged it quite necessary, and maybe even urgent, to go and see what Uni Park looked like after a night of combustion. So he'd go there that very morning, although he didn't therefore increase his pace, and he set out without manifesting the agitation appropriate only to rather obtuse souls who don't know how to defend themselves against the mobility of fate.

He followed his usual itinerary and, as was his wont, stopped in front of the ball bearings. He never missed this mechanical and amusing sight. Then he turned into the Avenue de Chaillot and the very first thing he noticed was that the chairoplane tower had disappeared. Some spots were still smoldering.

There were cops guarding the ruins. People were forming groups, the better to see and debate.

The stucco women had taken a hell of a bashing. In a single night they had aged fifty years; their chignons had come down and their tits were flopping over their thighs. Better still, they'd changed their race; their great, blackened posteriors had assumed a Hottentot steatopygia.

Like the chairoplane tower, the superstructure of the Alpinic Railway had collapsed.

Pierrot joined a group of commentators amongst whom he recognized a few philosophers. A fat fellow was saying to a little old man:

"It's a veritable catastrophe! And do *you* know, Monsieur, how it happened?"

"It seems that a short circuit . . ."

An individual who was chatting a bit farther away with great sweeping gestures rushed up:

"A likely tale, Monsieur! A likely tale! I saw it all. I live over there."

He indicated one of the directions in space.

"I saw it all, from my window," he went on. "It was arson."

They expected no less.

"This is what happened: I had a stomach upset last night, on account of eating some tinned stuff that couldn't have been fresh, some cassoulet. It gave me a migraine, not to mention an attack of colic, and as I couldn't sleep, I was half-suffocating, I went to my window, and my window, Monsieur, faces over there."

He indicated the same direction, more or less, as before.

"I have a splendid view over Uni Park. A splendid view, but it's noisy. Naturally all the lights were out. It was around three o'clock. I'm breathing in the beautiful evening air, it's doing me good, when all of a sudden the planes start revolving, they leave the ground and start flying around in a circle. I'm looking at them in surprise when, and this is the most extraordinary part, all of a sudden they burst into flames, it was a fine sight I can tell you: I couldn't get over it. But the best of all was when they came unhooked one after the other and nosedived down on to different parts of Uni Park, where they started fires all over the place. So help me, it was worth it, I'll say it was, good God. In no time at all, that magnificent amusement park was reduced to a blazing inferno. And a few seconds later it was a heap of embers in the middle of which with an infernal din, yes Messieurs, the turbulent, spiraloid network of the Russian Mountains collapsed. It was only at this moment that I realized I was witnessing one of the most terrible fires of modem times."

"Why?" asked Pierrot. "Did you think it was a flood at first?"

Everyone thought this repartee excellent, and Pierrot was all the more pleased with it in that he rarely managed to come out with such good ones. It wasn't in his character, and he'd just tossed this one off without really realizing what he was doing.

Having for a few moments envisaged the possibility of immediate and savage vengeance, such as smashing this individual's glasses and thirty-two teeth into smithereens, or triturating his mastoidean bone and saponifying his thymus, the witness, on reflection, contented himself with proceeding:

"You may laugh," he continued, "but you don't realize. It couldn't have been more impressive: flames as tall as houses, smoke all over the place, and then finally, and especially: it was a crime, it was arson, because you aren't going to tell me that those planes started up all by themselves and came unhooked all by themselves. I saw it myself, I wasn't dreaming."

As he seemed to be extremely hot-headed, the people listening to him didn't dare suggest any alternative versions, so they made comments on his. Who? Why? How? They expatiated. The director? An enemy? Vengeance? Profit? Complicity? They reminded each other of the incident at the Palace of Fun the day before. They considered various hypotheses, but someone found an objection to every one.

Pierrot listened, the interested onlooker, but then it suddenly occurred to him that he might make his own mind up about these events.

First he wanted to make sure that the house where Mademoiselle Pradonet lived had not been destroyed. He went back up the Boulevard Extérieur. Fire engines were still parked along the pavement and the firemen were spraying such shapeless debris as had the effrontery to be still burning.

Groups of onlookers were dotted about here and there; from time to time the police moved them on, and they stopped a little farther off. The fire hadn't reached the corner of the Avenue de la Porte-d'Argenteuil. Here too, animated discussions were going on. But nobody knew very much. Pierrot looked up, vaguely expecting to see Yvonne at a window but there was no one to be seen, not even a maid shaking her rugs. He continued his tour of Uni Park and, after the Avenue de la Porte-d'Argenteuil, turned into the Rue des Larmes. He had the satisfaction of observing that the chapel had been spared. Just as he was passing it he saw Mounnezergues coming out of his house. They recognized one another.

"Well, young man," he called out from the other side of the street, "what luck! The fire stopped a few meters before the tomb!"

He crossed the road and seized Pierrot's dexter hand, manifesting great cordiality.

"I saw the whole conflagration," he went on. "An awe-inspiring sight, Monsieur. I was worried about my prince, but the wind changed just at the right moment. The whole quadrilateral is in ashes, apart from this . . ." (He pointed to the chapel.) "You can imagine how delighted I am. Not that I congratulate myself on this catastrophe, although . . . Well, we'll talk about it some other time. I'll tell you my ideas on the subject. But what I wonder is: what is Pradonet going to do now? Pradonet, he's the director of Uni Park."

"I know," said Pierrot "I worked there."

"Goodness," said Mounnezergues. "What did you do?"

"I held the women over a blowhole in the Palace of Fun. But I was only there one evening. And another evening I was a fakir's assistant. That's all."

Mounnezergues seemed satisfied with this reply.

"The Palace of Fun," he remarked, "didn't someone already start to set fire to it yesterday evening?"

"So it seems. My two pals who were working with me were sacked."

"Ideas of revenge?"

Pierrot didn't understand. Mounnezergues noticed this.

"What do you think about it?" he asked him.

"About what?"

"About the fire?"

He pointed to the ruins of Uni Park.

"I couldn't care less," Pierrot replied.

He smiled because he had suddenly realized that if Yvonne didn't have to be at her stand she could, he hoped, go out with him from time to time, even if she went on seeing Paradis.

Mounnezergues insisted:

"Do you think it was natural, or was it deliberate?"

"I've no ideas on the subject."

And then, after reflection:

"In any case, it wasn't me," said Pierrot.

"Or me," said Mounnezergues, "although I might come under suspicion since I have a motive. But how could I have put it into practice? Perhaps a short circuit is sufficient explanation. Perhaps too we might suppose that Pradonet is in difficulties and is counting on the insurance money to rebuild his business?"

"I don't know anything about that," said Pierrot. "But about the way it happened, I heard a funny sort of guy, by the main entrance, claiming he'd seen how it was: according to him, the planes caught fire and came unhooked at full speed. And spread the fire. There's one thing I wonder, though, and that's what motive you could possibly have had to start the blaze."

"Oh! you can set your mind at rest about that, young man.

No court would ever accept that such a thought could lead to such extremes. I'm not talking about simple peace of mind, I must tell you about my relations with your ex-employer, but there's one thing that delights me, I'll tell you in confidence . . . this is my motive . . . But you must keep it to yourself. Do you swear?"

Pierrot spat on the ground.

"I swear," he said.

"Well then," said Mounnezergues, "now, Prince Luigi is going to be able to sleep in peace. Have you already considered the indecency there was in an amusement park coming and establishing itself by a tomb? From now on the prince's last sleep will no longer be disturbed by the loudspeakers' songs, the women's screams, and the machines' rumbles."

"But maybe Pradonet will rebuild it?" Pierrot suggested.

"In that case, you can see that it's no good as a motive! As for the tale about the fire-raising planes, that's just fantasy. I didn't see anything of the sort. Even though I was woken by the first flames. Yes, I think I'd been waiting for them for a long time. I was asleep with the window open on the Uni Park side. I was asleep, it must have been three, three-thirty. And the flames woke me, like the dawn and the cock crowing. But aeroplanes nosediving: no."

Pierrot, not knowing how to continue the conversation, said nothing. After a silence, Mounnezergues went on:

"The people who'd already tried to set fire to the Palace of Fun might also come under suspicion: that might have got them going. They'd acquired a taste for flames, you might say. Unfairly dismissed employees, like you and your friends, could come under suspicion. Or even a rival. Who knows? Mamar himself, whose circus has just taken up its pitch opposite. Actually, that reminds me; I must go and say hello to an old pal who works there. You come with me, young man. I'll introduce you to someone interesting, you'll make some contacts, you might even find work there. You aren't doing anything at the moment, are you?"

"No," said Pierrot. "I'm looking."

"Well then, come with me."

Mounnezergues had finished his daily rubbing down of the chapel and its circumjacent garden. He went home to put his utensils away and fetch his hat. Then he led Pierrot off. They went down the Rue des Larmes in the direction of the Avenue de Chaillot, which they crossed, after passing the ruins of the Uni Park Palais de Danse on their left.

At the Mamar Circus, everyone was calm. Mounnezergues went up to an employee who was brushing a zebra and asked him where he could find Psermis. The man told him that he had gone out, or rather that he hadn't yet arrived, because he was staying in a hotel. And Burmah, his assistant? He was attending to his animals.

"You don't know Psermis?" Mounnezergues asked Pierrot. "No? Haven't you ever been to the circus or the music hall, then?"

No. Pierrot mostly went to the movies. He had absolutely not the slightest idea who Psermis might be, and even less of an idea about Burmah, but he followed Mounnezergues as he went in search of him in a remote corner of the menagerie.

"Psermis is an old friend of mine," said Mounnezergues, "one of the very few, the only one. I knew him when he was spieling at the Anatomic Hall, which my father used to supply with waxworks. He couldn't have been more than eighteen but he already had God's own gift of the gab when it came to presenting his rubbish. And believe it or not, young man, I came across him later as a sergeant in the 3rd Zouaves, in which I did my military service, in Algeria. That was where he began to take an interest in training animals: he studied snake charmers and he himself taught a wild boar to walk on stilts, which no one had ever done before. This first success incited him to continue, and when he came back to France he adopted that profession. As you do not know, he became the most famous exhibitor of performing animals in both hemispheres. I say exhibitor, but he's been so successful that he can now afford simply to buy ready-trained animals."

At the entrance to the menagerie, a clown informed them that Burmah had just gone out. They about-turned.

"That's a nuisance," said Mounnezergues, "I'd have liked you to meet Psermis, he might even have found you a job. What would you say to working in a touring circus?"

"I'd rather stay in Paris," Pierrot replied. "But a temporary job, two or three weeks, that'd suit me fine, especially if it was round here."

He was thinking of Yvonne, naturally, she who lived so close.

"You mustn't be too demanding," said Mounnezergues.

Mounnezergues was now all set to consider Pierrot as his son. He had taken a liking to him. It had just come over him. Friendship is a passion like any other. For Mounnezergues was not lecherous either in body or mind. He looked at Pierrot out of the corner of his eye and stopped chattering. He was allowing an idea to germinate in him, an idea he would then cherish: that he would very much like Pierrot to succeed him as the guardian of Prince Luigi's tomb. In short, that he'd make him his heir.

Still pursuing this train of thought, Mounnezergues asked every circusite he came across whether he couldn't tell him where he, Mounnezergues, might have a chance of finding

Psermis. Several characters had no answer, but the Skeleton
Man informed them that there was some likelihood of their
doing so at The Faithful Coachman, a flunky's bistro at the corner of the Avenue de Chaillot and the Boulevard Victor-Marie-
Comte-Hugo. They didn't have to go all that way; not far from
the monument to Serpollet, they met Psermis. "There he is,"
said Mounnezergues, indicating a tall, greying, wiry-looking
fellow coming towards them with his hands in his pockets
whistling a jaunty air. Pierrot recognized the kook who had
been perorating outside the main entrance to Uni Park. "And
me that's already made an enemy of him," he thought, but he
hoped the fellow wouldn't recognize him.

"Psermis!" cried Mounnezergues, opening his arms.

The exhibitor of performing animals stopped both walking
and singing in order to examine the situation. A few moments
went by. Time was holding the two persons at the extremities
of a taut, extensile wire. It slackened its strain, and Psermis
dashed up to Mounnezergues. They embraced.

"Good old Mounnezergues!" said Psermis.

They thumped each other on the back and smiled profusely.

"Believe it or not," said Psermis, "I was meaning to come
and see you. I remembered you lived in this district. But I'd
lost your address. I was out of luck. Good old Mounnezergues.
Where are the 3rd Zouaves now, eh; and Constantine! Agi
mena! chouïa barka!"

He laughed heartily.

"And the camels, d'you remember? Good old Mounnezergues."

He looked at Pierrot.

"Is this your son?"

"No, not in the least. You know very well I'm not married."

Psermis, whispering in his ear, asked:

"A youthful indiscretion?"

"No, I tell you. He's a young Uni Park employee who enjoys my conversation."

"Well, he's out of a job now."

"Exactly. You wouldn't by any chance know of an opening for him with Mamar?"

Psermis considered the matter, or pretended to.

"I can't think of anything for the moment, but I'll let you know if there's anything going."

Having thus played the part of the employer in a style of classic purity, Psermis went back to where he started, and once again evoked Constantine, the 3rd Zouaves, and the camels in Biskra, a one-eyed place also known for its dates. With Mounnezergues feeding him his cues, it didn't take long before Pierrot was bored stiff. He managed to take his leave without too much difficulty, in spite of the great friendship Mounnezergues now manifested towards him which, however, was at the moment obumbrated by the insidious echoes of his youth.

"I'll let you know if I hear of anything," Psermis called after him.

Pierrot wondered how.

He walked off.

As it was more or less midday, the Uni Bar was indicated. Pierrot therefore walked back up the Boulevard Extérieur. People were still hanging around outside the Amusement Park. Others stood up in passing buses to get a look at the ruins, ashes and cinders.

Pierrot was hoping to see Paradis or Petit-Pouce, but neither was in the bistro. He made a tour of the establishment and then, having ordered an aperitif at the bar, took up his position in front of a pin-table and, having inserted his twenty sous therein, began to play. A group of habitues were chatting with the woman at the cash desk; naturally, they were talking about the fire. In front of the pari-mutuel man's cage, there was a queue of hippophiles.

Pierrot lost. No doubt the man who hired the machine out, seeing that people won too often, had come the day before and modified its level and filed down a few switches in the wrong direction. Pierrot didn't insist. He drank his aperitif, listening to the people's conversations, which didn't teach him a great deal, unless it was that some believed it was a short circuit, while others were saying that the police had the matter in hand.

As Paradis didn't appear any more than did Petit-Pouce, Pierrot lunched standing up: on a sandwich. He went and spent the rest of the day by the Seine; he even treated himself to a swimming bath and swam conscientiously. Both on his way there and on his way back, he squinted up at the windows of Pradonet's block, but didn't see anything interesting. That evening, at the Uni Bar, there was still no sign of his pals. Pierrot had dinner in a restaurant where they don't even put paper cloths on the tables, no doubt because their cuisine is said to be bourgeoise. He then treated himself to the movies (they happened to be showing *In Old Chicago*, the film about the fire, but this was a coincidence), then went back through the night to his hotel. During this journey, he thought, among other things, that it was high time he got his skates on and found a job. This thought was quicker than a flash, though, and he didn't dwell on it; and the rest of the time he thought a little about Yvonne and a lot about nothing.

During the following days, which were four, he made the same return journey between the hotel and the Argenteuil bridge and the Argenteuil bridge and the hotel, with a few detours around Uni Park. He didn't see Yvonne any more than he saw his friends, even though he looked for them, or Mounnezergues any more than Psermis, because he was avoiding them. It was on the evening of the fourth day, bereft of meeting and friendships, while he was slowly returning from the banks of the Seine where he had seen anglers and swimmers sharing a compact delight with so much moderation that there was still some left over for the truck drivers who, despite their strict schedule, pulled up at the corner of the bridge to drink their last glass of red wine before entering or leaving Paris, and while he was privately reflecting on this allegorical image, that Pierrot once again began to consider the flash that had struck him some time before, namely that it was time he got his skates on to earn his living, for he was fast running out of funds, and his main striking force against the pari-mutuel had been annihilated the day before by the imbecilic behavior of a trotter with long odds that had got nervous at the sight of a red umbrella and bolted. Having accepted this theoretical notion, the next thing was to proceed to its practical realization. Pierrot envisaged his possibilities: a distant cousin whom he went to see in similarly difficult circumstances would no doubt find him a job as a demonstrator at the Paris Fair; a former employer might take him on again to collect subscriptions to the Outer Suburbs Short-Term Insurance Company; the newspapers offered their columns of sits. vac. and wanted; various people might be visited. Pierrot decided that he'd rather go and see old Mounnezergues first.

Leaning on his elbows at his window, old Mounnezergues was smoking his pipe. Long-sighted, he had spotted Pierrot the moment he appeared at the corner of the Rue des Larmes and the Avenue de la Porte-d'Argenteuil, so he had had time to get his joy under control: he wanted to break the good

news calmly to the young man, the good news that he had
found him a little job that would be amusing to do. Pierrot,
who could also see well, thanks to the thickness of the lenses
in his glasses, had been conscious of being examined by
Mounnezergues, and began to walk even more nonchalantly
than usual. Nevertheless, when he had come within a reasonable distance he smiled amiably and raised two fingers to his
hat. Mounnezergues called out to him:

"Come on in! As it happens, I need to speak to you. Don't
bother to knock. The door's open. Come in on the right into
the garden and then along the corridor. I'll wait here for you."

"Thank you. Monsieur Mounnezergues," said Pierrot.

It's better to thank him in advance, thought Pierrot, who
was already seeing himself, and without enthusiasm, sweeping
up the dung in the Mamar ring. Although he wasn't obliged
to accept what Mounnezergues was going to offer him. As
he crossed the garden he had more or less made up his mind
not to let himself get involved with a traveling circus. As he
went into the house, he had quite made it up. That sort of
life, always on the move and away from Yvonne and the Porte
d'Argenteuil, didn't appeal to him in the least.

Mounnezergues was standing waiting for him at the end
of the corridor. He was smiling at him. Pierrot was surprised
to see how much younger he seemed to have got in so few
days. He went up to him, removing his felt hat politely but
with dignity.

"I was looking for work in other parts of town," he said,
"which is why I haven't been to see you the last few days."

Mounnezergues went on smiling at him, but didn't answer.
Pierrot stopped, not liking to hold out his hand, as this silence
seemed to portend a declaration of so important a nature as to
preclude the lowly banality of everyday greetings, but as he was

pretty sure that this declaration concerned his enrollment, his, Pierrot's, in the Mamar Circus, a traveling circus, he judged that this would be a sign of extreme tact on his part, and show that he would in no way be averse to following this establishment in its peregrinations, even though he was profoundly attached to his Parisian soil.

"The other day." he went on, with a feigned timidity that he considered the height of delicacy, "that gentleman who is your friend told you that he might perhaps know of a job for me . . . I came to see whether. . . Well, there's no work to be found in Paris at the moment . . . And as you seemed to take an interest in my situation, I came to see whether . . . whether . . ."

But Mounnezergues seemed quite determined, by his smiling mutism, to extract a fully-articulated petition from him. So Pierrot came out with it:

"I came to see whether there might not be a job for me in the Mamar Circus."

"Ah, there you are!" said a voice behind him. "I was wondering where you'd got to."

It was Mounnezergues. Pierrot turned round and saw him.

"That one," said Mounnezergues, pointing to the dummy, "I made that one about ten years ago, to amuse myself. Funny sort of amusement, you'll say. But come on in."

Pierrot comes on in, quite pleased to have carried on a conversation for at least a few moments with a waxwork.

"What'll you have?" asked Mounnezergues. "A kirsch?"

"With pleasure," said Pierrot.

There was a big portrait on the wall in front of him.

"Prince Luigi," said Mounnezergues, filling two little glasses. "It's an enlargement of a photo that was published in the papers at the time. It's a good likeness. It was done by an artist. I once had the idea of making a wax model of his head.

It turned out very well. I kept it for maybe three months, and then I melted it down, I considered it showed a lack of respect for the prince. But that's not what I wanted to talk about. Is my kirsch good?"

"Yes, Monsieur Mounnezergues."

"Monsieur Mounnezergues? No need to call me monsieur. But this is what it's about, and why I'm glad to see you. I've found you a little job, only a few days but that's still something, and then, it will amuse you. I'm sure of that."

Only a few days, he wouldn't mind that.

"Thank you," said Pierrot "Thank you, Monsieur Mounnezergues."

"Don't call me monsieur, for heaven's sake!" cried Mounnezergues.

Pierrot was now curious to know what on earth Mounnezergues might consider "amusing"—at least for him, Pierrot. But the doorbell rang.

Mounnezergues leant out of the window to see who it was.

"It's Pradonet," he said to Pierrot.

"Right, I'll go," said Pierrot. "I'll come back some other time."

"No no, my boy, don't go, you aren't in my way."

And he hurried off to open the door.

Pierrot went to the window in his turn. From this slightly raised ground floor level, he could see not only the peaceful chapel encaged in its rectangular square but also the extensive terrain of cinders and ashes that represented the existing state of Uni Park. Twisted, charred, recharred, and menacing the heavens, the Alpinic Railway girders alone laid claim to some sort of tragic grandeur. The rest looked no more annihilated than it had at the time when it was functioning under the designation of attractions, and remained almost as agreeable to

look at, especially if you added the charm of the game of iden-
tifications: that was So-and-so's machine, that was the fortune
teller's booth. Pierrot was trying to find the site of Yvonne's
stand when Pradonet came into the room. He turned around.

"Come on in," said Mounnezergues, "and don't take any
notice of this young man. We can talk in front of him. A glass
of kirsch?"

"With great pleasure," said Pradonet.

Having examined Pierrot, who had nodded a polite greeting to him, he added:

"I have a feeling I've met him somewhere, this boy." And
to Pierrot:

"Haven't I already seen you somewhere else, young man?
I'm Pradonet, the director of Uni Park."

"I was employed there," said Pierrot. "Maybe that was
where you saw me."

"Maybe," said Pradonet.

He examined Pierrot once again, but without managing to
form an opinion. Then he turned to Mounnezergues:

"I have serious things to say to you, Mounnezergues."

"I'm listening," said Mounnezergues. "Just try my kirsch."

"This young man bothers me," said Pradonet. "Couldn't
you tell him to go away?"

"I'll go, Monsieur Mounnezergues," said Pierrot

"No no, you stay, son," said Mounnezergues, who added
for Pradonet's benefit: "You can talk in front of him, he's my
adopted son, I have nothing to hide from him."

This declaration staggered Pradonet. It silenced him for a
few moments, while he wondered whether this might bring
about any modification in their respective positions.

"Properly adopted?" he asked Mounnezergues. "Is he your
heir?"

"No doubt."

"But only a year ago you assured me that you didn't have any heirs."

"Well, I have one now."

"No, no, no!" cried Pradonet. "I'm not falling for that. You've always strung me along about that bit of ground by assuring me that you had no heirs and now all of a sudden here's one sprung from goodness knows where."

"That," said Mounnezergues, "is my business. My private life is no concern of yours, is it? All I can do is advise you to take the said heir into account when making your plans."

"You have a funny way of going about things," said Pradonet, beginning to give Pierrot some furious looks.

Pierrot smiled at him amiably.

"By the way," said Mounnezergues, "what about that fire?"

"You saw it, eh?" said Pradonet very proudly. "What a catastrophe! The whole lot went up in flames. There's nothing left."

"It's a terrible blow for you," said Mounnezergues.

"Yes indeed," said Pradonet. "Especially at the beginning of the season, it's a calamity. But I'm insured."

"Will the insurance company pay?" asked Mounnezergues.

"Why shouldn't it? They're investigating at the moment. But I don't care what the result is. I shall get paid."

"You don't seem particularly interested in knowing why Uni Park burned down." Mounnezergues remarked.

"There, Mounnezergues, you are wrong. I've even given the matter a lot of thought."

"And what have you come up with?"

"Nothing," said Pradonet. "In any case, it wasn't me, and the insurance will pay, and with that and some other money I shall build a Uni Park that will no longer be a fair but a monument, and that's why I've come to see you, Mounnezergues.

Because for my monument to be a real monument, it has to be square, and for it to be square, I have to have your land, Mounnezergues, and to demolish your prince's chapel."

"No," said Mounnezergues.

"Listen to me, Mounnezergues. The future Uni Park will have seven floors, and floors six meters high. There'll be attractions, machines, and everything, on every floor. And an Alpinic Railway will run through the whole establishment. And on the terrace there'll be a swimming pool, a Palais de Danse and a parachute tower. But all that is absolutely nothing, let me tell you, beside everything I'm still going to think up. So the whole outfit will be unique, people will come to Paris especially to see it, there won't be anything like it in the entire world, and just because of a Poldevian prince you'd be prepared to prevent the realization of this project? And deprive Paris of its greatest curiosity? No, Mounnezergues, you aren't going to do that. For me, for Paris, for France, I ask you this favor."

"Nuts," said Mounnezergues.

"You're a . . ." said Pradonet. "You're a . . ." said Pradonet. "You're a . . ." said Pradonet, "madman. Yes, a madman."

He had stood up and was flailing his great arms around at the risk of breaking various knickknacks or knocking down Prince Luigi's portrait. Then he sat down again and drank his kirsch.

"Not bad," he said, very calmly. "At all events, Mounnezergues, think over my proposition. I'll pay you two-hundred-thousand francs, half in cash, the other half in six months. All right?"

"Oh no," said Mounnezergues.

Pradonet sighed.

He looked dreamily at his empty glass, then stood up. He shook Mounnezergues's hand, saying, "We'll talk about it further," and he also shook Pierrot's hand absentmindedly.

He took his leave.

While he was waiting for Mounnezergues to come back after showing his visitor out, Pierrot once again looked at Prince Luigi's portrait. It was a fine work of art, a very good likeness no doubt, every hair on his head and in his eyelashes beautifully delineated, every bit as good as a photo. As for the subject himself, he must have been a handsome lad, with nevertheless a touch of the dago about him. On reflection, Pierrot didn't find him especially likeable, and it was only when he remembered that this poor young man had died in the prime of life, and from a stupid accident, that he forgave him his side-whiskers, his too-swarthy eyes and his Argentina-brilliantined hair, and was willing to accept the fact that Mounnezergues guarded his tomb with such perfect although inexplicable fidelity.

"Poor boy, eh?" said Mounnezergues, who had come back. "Dying like that in the prime of life, how sad! You are probably wondering how I can be so attached to someone whom I only knew when he was dying, to the point of sacrificing a tidy sum of money to him—you saw how I sent old Pradonet packing, at least my reply was clear!—well . . . what was I saying?"

"You were imagining that it amazed me to see you so devoted to the cause of the repose of the soul of the Poldevian princes."

"Why 'imagining'? Isn't that what you were thinking?"

"Oh, I'm not nosy. It's like your conversation with Pradonet, if you'd rather I never heard it, that's how it is. I haven't the slightest recollection of it, now, if that suits you."

Mounnezergues looked at Pierrot seriously.

"You're another strange fellow. But in any case, I want to tell you that if you would have liked me to answer the question I imagined you wanted to ask, well, I had no answer to give you. There."

"And besides, I didn't come to annoy you," said Pierrot.

"You're nice," said Mounnezergues absentmindedly.

He was thinking.

"Ah!" he exclaimed. "And your job! Pradonet interrupted us. Are you interested?"

"Oh yes, I'm sure I am," said Pierrot. "But what does it consist of?"

"Didn't I tell you?"

"It would only last a few days, that's what you told me."

"That's right. It's this. First of all: have you got a driving license?"

"Naturally."

"I thought as much. Can you drive a van?"

"And how," said Pierrot.

"Well, this is what you'll have to do. I told you about Psermis. You even saw him. I told you that he exhibits performing animals. He buys them from trainers, mainly from Voussois, who lives in the Midi. Sometimes the animals don't suit him. That's what has happened with the last batch he sent. Your job will be to take those animals back to Voussois and bring back a batch of new subjects for Psermis. Mamar is lending him a van. That's what you'll be driving. In short, you're being offered a little trip."

"And I'll be paid for that?"

"Handsomely, even. But it'll only employ you for about a week."

"That's better than nothing," said Pierrot, who thereupon experienced the feeling called gratitude.

At this moment, he was naturally not thinking about Mounnezergues's inheritance.

7

A FEW DAYS LATER, on the Route Nationale Xbis, Pierrot was driving at as good a pace as was possible for the Mamar Circus van. He had left Paris around seven and was hoping to get to Butanges for lunch. Now that he'd left the suburbs behind him, he was breathing in the good holiday and country air, even though it was constantly vitiated by the multifarious cars and trucks whose average speed was superior to his, and they were many. Nevertheless, he felt full of joy and hummed "the air is pure the road is wide," and "soup and beef and beans." By his side, Mésange, his cap on the back of his head, and well wrapped up in a goatskin, was taking a keen interest in the landscape ahead of him. From time to time he turned round to Pierrot, who then treated him to his most charming smile. By Mésange's side, Pistolet, leaning on the door, was also carefully examining the landscape he was being offered. In the back of the van, finally, tranquillity radiated its silence, and, even at level crossings or rather too hunchbacked humpbacked bridges, Pierrot heard no incipient protest therein. As he only just knew how to drive, he was not displeased that his van was just an old banger, as this enabled him to put his foot right down on the accelerator without exceeding forty kilometers an hour. He found himself constantly being passed, but with neither hate nor envy, and he exulted silently in everything he found pleasant that presented itself to his sight: the road when it's nice and straight, and the road when it curves, the roadmen and the spinneys, the calm little villages, and the philosophical cows in their pastures. Not counting Mésange and Pistolet, whom he found infinitely agreeable.

At around midday he was still a good long way from Butanges. He stopped in the countryside to go and have a pee against a tree, and at the same time to do some thinking, while consulting his map. It was obvious that he was going to be behind schedule, so he decided to stop for lunch at the next place on his route, which was called Saint-Mouézy-sur-Eon. There, opposite the old covered market, he found an inn that looked suitable, and behind a gigantic truck he parked his vehicle. He examined its contents: no one in it was any the worse for the journey, but everyone in it was hungry. Pierrot consulted the bit of paper Psermis had given him, distributed the rations according to the instructions received, and was careful not to forget to provide something to drink. During this time, mitocans and mocofans, kids or adults, had discovered the presence of Mésange, who had moved over behind the steering wheel: they didn't quite know what to think, but were getting ready to laugh.

When he'd finished attending to his dumb friends, Pierrot went into the bistro, and, having made salutations to the assembled company, inquired about the possibility of a meal. But of course they could nourish him. He reserved a table for three and went to fetch his two traveling companions, who jumped down merrily. The crowd manifested equal joy. An imperious silence fell as they entered the café, and everyone was staggered to see the three of them taking their places at the table.

Pierrot sat down in front of his plate with great satisfaction: he was really hungry. Mésange, having thrown his pelisse into a corner, sat down opposite him and Pistolet took possession of the third chair, at the end of the table, between the two of them. The people looking at them (apart from the waitress moving up and down the room and a heavy-jowled matron whose blubber was wobbling behind the counter) were: the driver of the gigantic truck with his acolyte, a uniformed delivery man from a department store with his driver (Pierrot hadn't noticed their vehicle), a cyclist who hadn't taken off the clips gripping the bottom of his trouser legs, and a fat gentleman who probably lived in the district and who looked as if he was going hunting. All these people, then, were looking at the trio without saying a word. Pierrot pretended to be unaware of their sustained attention.

The waitress came up to him.

"Is it for lunch?" she asked, in a voice touched with emotion.

"No," said Pierrot, "it's for dinner. But we're going to have dinner early today, in other words now."

Mésange seemed to appreciate the joke, and cast a both lascivious and facetious glance in the waitress's direction, which discomfited her. She stammered:

"Very well, Monsieur."

Pierrot examined the menu and asked:

"Is all this still on?"

"Yes, Monsieur."

"Well then," said he, "hors d'oeuvres varies for us all. After that, for me, tripe, for Monsieur" (he pointed to Mésange) "gigot with kidney beans. That all right for you?" he asked him. (Mésange thumped the table lightly with his fist several times, a clear sign of consent) "And for him" (Pierrot pointed to Pistolet), "a nice soup with croutons and some turnips, a double portion, he's a vegetarian. Isn't that right old pal?" he asked Pistolet. who didn't answer, being no doubt indifferent to this kind of categorization.

The waitress stayed there without budging, like an idiot.

"A nice bottle of red for me," Pierrot added, "and some water for these gentlemen."

The waitress departed in a daze. She went over to the proprietress.

Meanwhile, Pierrot was rubbing his hands in satisfaction. Mésange was actively wiping his plate, and Pistolet, having managed to get hold of the salt shaker, was absorbing its contents little by little.

Soon the waitress came back, the bearer of a message. Which she formulated thus:

"We don't mind serving you lunch," she said to Pierrot, "but Madame says she's never going to allow animals to eat out of china that's for people."

"Don't be such a dope," said Pierrot.

"No, but look here," was what the maid said.

"But yes, dope. Just go and tell your boss that the three of us are going to eat here, with all the respect due to us, and in proper china, not in feeding troughs, and that's that. I'm paying."

He tapped himself on the chest, in the region of his wallet.

"'S'not for you that she says that," the waitress insisted, "it's on account of them. You catch diseases from animals, that's for sure."

"And you," retorted Pierrot in a low voice, "what animal did you catch your pox from?"

He pinched her bottom, and Mésange undid her apron strings, thus reinventing in a flash of genius the gag commonly practiced in hostelries for the common soldier.

"Come on then," said Pierrot, "serve us pronto, and no more messing about."

She departed once again, but this time in the direction of the kitchen, where the proprietor was rushing around. Mésange watched her vanish behind the door and then, turning back to Pierrot, he held out his hand to him, no doubt to congratulate him on the energy of his remarks and the firmness of his rejoinder. Naturally, Pierrot shook it. The rest of the room remained silent and almost motionless: astonishment could be read on every feature of their physiognomy, and stupefaction down to the tip of their noses. Outside, there was a great crush of young rubbernecks against the windows. Mésange saw them and pulled a few faces for their benefit; and anyway, it hadn't taken him long to despise them. He then set about sampling the mustard pot, but the first spoonful seemed to him to demonstrate that this substance owed its origin to the acerbity of some practical joker, and he made as if to project the receptacle through a mirror in which the antics of an image seemed to indicate the presence of a second Mésange. Pierrot restrained him just in time. But Mésange, deprived of this pleasure, gave him a ferocious look, which boded no good. Pierrot immediately located a water carafe and had quite made up his mind to bash Mésange's brains in if he carried out the evil intentions he seemed to be conceiving. Luckily the waitress appeared from the kitchen with the hors d'oeuvres; Mésange's attention was diverted, his bad temper dispersed, and Pierrot salivated joyfully. Pistolet, during this time, had remained perfectly calm.

"I brought hors d'oeuvres for everyone," said the serving wench.

"That's precisely what I asked you to do," retorted Pierrot, beginning to serve his two companions, although putting only vegetal substances on Pistolet's plate.

Mésange, skillfully wielding knife and fork, went to work on his portion with gusto, as did Pierrot. Pistolet, having first sniffed at his plate suspiciously, cast a circular glance at those present (not without causing them some disquiet), examined the maid from head to foot with a somber, beady eye, and finally took the plunge. And the celeriac and the radishes were heard crunching under his powerful, yellowish teeth.

"What's your name?" Pierrot asked the girl, who was still standing there in a daze, gawping at the trio.

"Mathurine, Monsieur." she replied.

"Well then, Mathurine." said Pierrot, "push off, we want to be left in peace. Got it? When we want the next course, we'll ring."

"Very well, Monsieur." said she, and she fled.

The spectators took this as applying to them, too, and pretended to adopt a normal, casual attitude. And in any case, the two guys from the gigantic truck, having finished their chasers, paid and left. Two rather ill-defined characters came in and shared a bottle while conducting a discussion, seeming not to notice Pierrot's table. All this restored every appearance of normality to the room. Then Mathurine brought the tripe and the gigot and beans and, for Pistolet, some soup and turnips. Later, they cut into some cheese, and the meal was completed with fruit. Pierrot had coffee, but the others didn't. Mésange accepted this privation with good grace, for he didn't like it; the embargo on wine he found harder to bear, for he was only allowed reddened water. As for Pistolet, he showed no signs of bellyaching.

Pierrot, as he emptied his bottle of red, felt his interior

twilight traversed from time to time by philosophical fulgu-
rations, such as: "Life is worth living," or: "Existence has its
good sides"; and, on another theme: "Life is funny," or "What
a strange thing existence is." A few sentimental rockets (the
memory of Yvonne) flew up to the greatest heights and then
descended in showers of sparks. A poetic projector, finally, occasionally swept this sky with its metaphorical paintbrush, and
Pierrot, looking at the scene opening out before him, said to
himself: "It's like the movies." And he smiled at his two companions, who definitely seemed to be finding him more and
more likeable. After all, they had only known each other since
the morning.

Just as Mathurine was bringing the coffee, the boss came
out of his kitchen, and, after greeting the cyclist and the two
delivery men (he knew them, no doubt), made his way over
to the three representatives of the Mamar Circus with a res-
olute step.

"Well then," he asked Pierrot, "it all right?"

"Not bad, not bad," said Pierrot.

"And . . . these gentlemen . . . are they satisfied?"

"Are you satisfied?" Pierrot asked them.

They both swung their heads from high to low.

"Well, that's good," said the innkeeper. "It's not every day
that I have the honor to cater for distinguished guests. Allow
me to offer you a glass of kirsch. Mathurine! The bottle of
kirsch, the one I keep for myself, and two glasses."

"It'll be difficult not to offer one to Mésange," said Pierrot.
"I'd rather not upset him."

"Three glasses," called the innkeeper.

"Pistolet, though, is a naturist: neither meat nor alcohol."

The innkeeper took a chair and sat down next to Pistolet,
who inspired more confidence in him than Mésange, who was
observing him through screwed-up eyes.

"Is that your van outside?"

"Yes."

"Do you belong to the Mamar Circus?"

"Yes."

Mathurine brought the kirsch. They drank. Mésange didn't think it bad. The innkeeper had the glasses refilled.

"Where is it at the moment, then, the Mamar Circus?" asked the innkeeper.

"At the Porte de Chaillot, opposite Uni Park. Which was burned down, the papers talked about it."

"I saw that," said the innkeeper. "A catastrophe. Were any of the houses round about destroyed?"

"No It was only the booths and the attractions that went up."

"Do you know the district?"

"And how," said Pierrot.

Pistolet, bored by the conversation, had fallen asleep. Mésange had taken a cigar out of his pocket, had lit it, and was smoking placidly.

"You know the little cafe at the corner of the Rue des Larmes and the Avenue de la Porte-d'Argenteuil?" asked the innkeeper.

"No," Pierrot replied. "There isn't one."

"There isn't one there now, then?" said the innkeeper. "The Café Posidon? That's my name."

"No," said Pierrot. "It doesn't exist anymore. It's a garage now."

"I thought as much," said the innkeeper. "Everything changes fast on this earth. Nothing lasts. Everything you saw when you were young, when you're old it's disappeared. You never wash your feet twice in the same water. If you say it's daytime, a few hours later it's nighttime, and if you say it's nighttime, a few hours later it's daytime. Nothing lasts, everything moves. Don't you get tired of it, finally? But it's true, you're too young to understand that, although you only have to run through your memories and you very soon find everything buggering off around you, or that it has buggered off. But . . . is it really true that the Café Posidon doesn't exist any more?"

"Like I told you. It's funny, that, you having lived in the district. What a coincidence! Personally, I know it very well, that district."

"I kept a bistro there for twenty years. I gave it up five or six years ago."

"Then you must know the chapel!" Pierrot exclaimed.

"What chapel?" asked Posidon.

"The Poldevian chapel, of course, in the Rue des Larmes, behind Uni Park."

"I can't place it," said Posidon.

"There's a little square around it."

"I can't place it."

"It doesn't matter," said Pierrot.

"Are you sure there's a chapel in that street?"

"It doesn't matter," said Pierrot.

He asked for the bill, and paid. As Mathurine was withdrawing, taking her tip, Mésange undid her apron strings for the second time.

"Even so, it's a queer coincidence," said Pierrot, "that you used to live in those parts."

"But it's strange, that chapel, I can't place it . . ."

Pierrot shook his hand and woke up Pistolet, who jumped down from his chair.

Mésange had gone to fetch his pelisse.

"Evening, all," said Pierrot.

They left, all three of them, and soon the van was once again driving along the road to Butanges, which it passed through at around four in the afternoon. At five, it entered the Scribe Forest, from which it emerged at six. At seven, they were in Antony, a big industrial town. Pierrot decided to carry on and to spend the night at Saint-Flers-sur-Caillavet. He stopped outside a certain Hôtel du Cheval Blanc, which looked as if it corresponded to his social situation. Having put his vehicle in the garage and inspected its cargo, which seemed to be in good condition and to be withstanding the wear and tear of the journey quite satisfactorily, he went in search of the landlord, who turned out to be a tall, thin woman, thinner than thin, who was balancing up her cash behind a counter that was two-thirds glassed in. At Pierrot's request for a room with two beds, the lady, hearing a commotion in the lower regions, straightened up in her seat and leaned out of her aquarium. She saw Mésange and Pistolet. She was in no way astonished. Mésange saluted her by raising his hat with great dignity. Pistolet, totally indifferent, gazed at her with his somber, beady eye.

"What about him?" she asked, pointing at him with a thin, knotted finger.

"For him," Pierrot replied, "I'd like a mattress."

"Is he clean?"

"As clean as you and me," Pierrot replied.

She gave a skeletal laugh, which was rather difficult to interpret.

"Oh, you know," she said, "at my age, nothing surprises me any more."

"I have no such intention," said Pierrot. "Come to that," he added, "what age?"

"What a wag," she retorted.

She pressed a bell. A maid appeared; she uttered a little scream when she saw the three companions.

"Number 43 for these gentlemen," her employer told her, "with an extra mattress."

She asked Pierrot:

"Are you going to have dinner here?"

"And how," Pierrot replied. "I could eat a horse. And my pals too . . . Isn't that right, boys?"

Mésange reacted joyously to the prospect of nosh by executing a supple, elegant movement that left him sitting on the desk. He immediately undertook to make a thorough study of the nature of a particular inkwell by sticking his fingers into it. Pistolet had sat down on his behind and was patiently awaiting meal and mattress; he had absolute confidence in Pierrot.

Nothing daunted, the lady offered Mésange a piece of blotting paper, for him, on it, to wipe his hands. Which he did, very intelligently.

"Oh no," said the lady, resuming the conversation at a previous stage, "I'm too old to get excited by any monkey business. Just think, Monsieur, that during the three years of its existence, I was a cashier at l'Admirable's Gallery in Uni Park, in Paris."

No doubt about it, said Pierrot to himself, someone has deliberately strewn this route with people who used to live in that district.

"It doesn't exist anymore," he said.

"I know. Alas, when you get to a certain age there isn't much left of what you knew in your youth."

No doubt about it, said Pierrot to himself, they're all the same.

"You're too young to have visited l'Admirable's Gallery," the lady went on. "Apart from the stock exhibits like the Bearded Woman and the Skeleton Man . . ."

"I've met that one," Pierrot interrupted.

"Which one? The Mamar Circus one?"

"Yes."

"I couldn't stand him. He was that pretentious. The last time the Mamar Circus came to these parts he came to say hello to me, Pautrot, that's his name. I wasn't particularly pleased to see him again. Between you and me, he had a crush on me, he was even quite far gone. But myself, I'd never been able to stomach him. Antipathies, there's no explaining them, don't you think?"

"Of course," said Pierrot, who immediately went on to inquire about the location of the hotel restaurant.

Mésange was becoming impatient and was starting to devour the blotting paper offered gratuitously by the management.

The proprietress let them go. And they entered a room in which there were about a dozen tables equipped with cloths, flowers, and electroplated objects. "This is going to cost me quite a bit," said Pierrot to himself. And then: "So what; I did at least choose the most modest. I'll just be that much less in pocket." As for Mésange. he was manifestly impressed by this luxury. Not Pistolet. however: he would have behaved just as naturally at the Ritz as in the lowest of low dives.

There was no one in the restaurant but an NCO in the Spahis, whose brilliant uniform greatly intrigued Mésange; this NCO was in the company of a heavily-made-up moll. At the far end, though, there was a gentleman on his own displaying a thick neck and a massive back; he didn't condescend to turn round. As for the soldier and his bird, they were so absorbed in one another that they didn't waste too much time on studying the new arrivals. As for the waiter, he adopted a disgusted air; nevertheless, he performed his duties with abnegation. When they had finished their meal, Pierrot left him a big tip.

The soldier and his conquest had gone. Pistolet was dozing. Mésange was smoking his vesperal cigar rather irritably; it was his bedtime. Pierrot was finishing a cigarette, vaguely wondering what sort of a night he was going to have with these two specimens in the same room. At the same time, he was surprised that the gentleman at the other end of the room, who had been paying his bill when they arrived, was still hanging around, yet without showing any curiosity. Pursuing his investigations in this direction, he noticed that a particular mirror must have informed the personage as to his, Pierrot's, identity; he completed these observations by a thorough examination of the individual's dorsum. The result of all these cogitations was that: he knew the guy.

He then made a series of signs to Mésange, with eye and hand. Mésange understood admirably (but what is it not possible to communicate by gestures? what a superfluous luxury is the use of the vocal cords!—such were the heights to which Pierrot's thought then rose). Mésange put his cigar down delicately in the saucer he was using as an ashtray, got down from his chair and, with a lithe, loping step, made his way towards the solitary man at the far end.

He approached him silently.

He grabbed hold of one of the legs of the gentleman's chair, and with a powerful grasp, pulled it towards him. Rather like those waiters who, with a sudden jerk, remove a tablecloth and leave the table still laid. The gentleman remained suspended in the air for a few fragments of a second. Then he fell. He got to his feet, swearing, while Mésange phlegmatically went back to his place. His cigar hadn't had time to go out. He picked it up again and enjoyed a long puff.

"Well," said Pierrot, "so we don't recognize our pals anymore?"

Petit-Pouce finally showed his face.

"You and your idiotic practical jokes," he said to Pierrot.

"It's you I'm talking to," he immediately added, addressing Pierrot.

It was out of prudence that he had specified the intentionality of his sentence, because Mésange had given him a frowning look.

"Were you hiding from me?" Pierrot asked.

"I hadn't seen you," said Petit-Pouce, who had now decided to take the thing as a joke. "Is it safe to sit down at your table?"

"They're splendid little pals," said Pierrot, and he made the introductions: "Pistolet . . . Petit-Pouce . . . Mésange . . . Petit-Pouce . . ."

"How're you making out, then?" asked Petit-Pouce.

"We're earning our modest living," said Pierrot. "And you?"

"We're doing the best we can," replied Petit-Pouce. "By the way, hey, it seems Uni Park's gone up in flames?"

"Yes. Nothing left of it. But it was already finished for you, as well as for me."

"It didn't take you long to find another job. Funny sort of job, anyone might think."

"There's no such thing as a foolish trade," said Pierrot.

"What's it actually consist of?"

Pierrot wondered for an instant what he ought to answer, but Petit-Pouce didn't give him time:

"I see. I see . . . But I didn't know you had that particular gift."

"One does what one can," Pierrot replied modestly. "What about you? You haven't told me anything."

Petit-Pouce leaned over towards him and murmured:

"I'm on an investigation."

Mésange had also leaned over to hear better.

"So you're in the secret police now?" Pierrot asked.

"No. No. Private police."

Mésange threw himself back, stubbed his cigar out in the saucer and forthwith devoured the butt, all the while keeping a severe eye on Petit-Pouce. Pistolet, who had no doubt also been antagonized by Petit-Pouce's whispering, scratched his chin against a corner of the table and then began to wander around the room silently.

"Naturally," said Pierrot, "you can't tell me what your investigation is."

"Naturally," Petit-Pouce acquiesced. "It's confidential, you understand."

"Is it anything to do with any people I know?"

"No."

"Do I know anyone who knows them?"

"Yes. Me, for example."

This made them laugh. The waiter, annoyed at seeing them still there such a long time after paying their bills, requested them to move into the coffee room. They stood up.

"I'll take them up to bed," said Pierrot to Petit-Pouce, "and then come and join you. We'll have a drink together."

"Right," said Petit-Pouce.

Pierrot went up to the room reserved for them and was amazed to see the promised mattress. Pistolet immediately understood that it was destined for him and forthwith curled up on it. Doesn't even say goodnight. Shuts his eyes and falls asleep. But putting Mésange to bed presented some difficulties; having undressed, Mésange tried one bed, then the second, went back to the first, and started bouncing from one bed to the other. Without being particularly fastidious, Pierrot nevertheless felt reluctant to sleep in the same sheets as this energumen, so he thought about having recourse to the big stick; on reflection, though, he decided in favor of flight and left the room abruptly, switching the light off behind him. He locked the door.

Downstairs, the coffee room was deserted. Or almost. The proprietress was engaged in some kind of activity behind the cash desk.

"Excuse me, Madame," said Pierrot to this person, "you haven't seen the gentleman on his own who was dining in the restaurant just now, have you?: a not very tall gentleman, fairly well built . . ."

"I know the one. No, he's gone."

"Isn't he staying here?"

"No, Monsieur. Did you want to speak to him?"

"Yes. He was supposed to be waiting for me. He was a pal. I wonder why he didn't wait for me."

"He's what they call unreliable."

"We used to work together at Uni Park."

At that, the lady deigned to show some animation. She inquired about dates; she couldn't have known Pierrot, even though he claimed to have aged outrageously in the service; as for Petit-Pouce, at whose seniority he made an approximate guess, she didn't remember him.

"I'd have recognized him," she said. "I'm eagle-eyed."

"He's in the police now," said Pierrot.

And he suddenly realized that there might be some connection between Petit-Pouce's mission and the existence of this lady. But she didn't seem put out.

"I know," she said calmly. "He told me all about it. He's looking for a girl, the one Pradonet's mistress's first lover killed himself for. What a business! He's investigating on behalf of the widow Prouillot. But he hasn't discovered anything. It's his opinion, even, that the woman never existed. I hadn't asked him any questions."

"No?" said Pierrot.

"No. Do *you* know her, the widow Prouillot?"

"Not specially."

"A funny woman. I wonder what she can be thinking about the Uni Park fire. And Pradonet? What on earth can he be saying!"

"He has plans."

"Who told you so?"

"He did."

"*He* did?"

The lady was most amazed. Pierrot was putting her down. He explained Pradonet's plan to her.

"But," he concluded, "the Poldevian chapel is preventing him from rounding off his square."

"What's that, the Poldevian chapel?" the ex-cashier of l'Admirable's Gallery asked absently.

He gave her some topographical data, but she hadn't the slightest recollection of ever having seen the thing. What she was interested in was Pradonet.

"All things considered," she said, "it could have been him that set fire to the joint."

"There's an inquiry," said Pierrot. "Did you know him well, Pradonet?"

"You're asking *me* that? *me?* A charming man, scrupulous! subtle! witty! modest."

"Capable of starting a fire?" asked Pierrot.

"When people have their reasons, they're capable of anything," said the landlady, standing up, closing her cash desk, and putting out various lights.

"Good night, Madame."

He went up to his room, somewhat disappointed by the abrupt end brought to this conversation. But by the time he had reached his floor, the second, he had anyway managed to persuade himself that Pradonet's psychology was none of his business, any more than it was that of his landlady. He opened the door to his room and was immediately assailed by the pungent fragrance of wild beast that was floating in thick layers in the atmosphere of the room, a pathetic odor of suppressed colic. Mésange had shut the window, no doubt to avoid the temptation of going for a walk on the roofs. He was sleeping peacefully, as was Pistolet. An empty bed awaited Pierrot, even though it had been slightly crumpled by Mésange. He tottered over to the window and opened it quietly. The pure air went to his head. The little town was dead to the world, under a sprinkling of stars. The classic train emitted its well-known call.

Pierrot realized that he couldn't spend the night there. But he was extremely tired, and he imagined that he might rest for a time on one of the benches in the square surrounding the town hall. He closed the window and went downstairs. To get out, he had to disturb a night porter, who gave him a dirty look.

Once outside, he observed that the temperature was mild, and that it wouldn't be too unpleasant to sleep in the open air. He tried to get his bearings, but when he saw a signpost directing him to the station he followed its advice, abandoning at least temporarily his first intention; he imagined that somewhere there he might find a café or buffet open where he could drink some sort of liquid that would disinfect his nostrils; he also told himself that if Petit-Pouce was trying to avoid him at all costs, he was maybe going to catch a night train; in which case he, Pierrot, might well catch up with him. It wasn't that he was particularly interested in the exploits of that character but, just to see what happened, he could always mention the hotel landlady who had worked at Uni Park and who might possibly be the cause of Petit-Pouce's presence here.

But outside the station, everything was just as dark and heavy with silence as it was in the rest of the town; Pierrot crossed the square; an employee told him that the express train to Paris had left twenty minutes before and that no more trains would be leaving until dawn. In the waiting rooms there was only a group of Kabyles, no Petit-Pouce. The railwayman showed him how to get back to the town hall.

This silence, this darkness, these narrow streets, all inclined Pierrot to think of nothing in particular, for example of vague calculations about the time it might well finally be shortly. He looked to his right, to his left, as if trying to latch on to some interesting little oddment here or there, but found nothing— at best, the shop signs, but they were nothing like so good as the ball bearings in the Avenue de Chaillot. For a moment, remembering his military life, he thought of visiting the cat-house of this sub-prefecture, but he didn't meet anyone who could tell him where to find it. Finally, he got lost. He was now crossing a little industrial suburb, with small factories here and there. One was lit up, and machines were whirring inside it. Farther on, Pierrot came to a widish road with a double row of trees, maybe a main road? maybe a secondary one? He went on walking for a few moments.

He heard a loud scream quite near him, a woman's scream, a frightened scream.

His very first thought, as the first immediately feasible possibility, was to run like hell in the opposite direction. But, having given due consideration to the feminine origin of this clamor, he plucked up courage and looked. There were heaps of stars in the sky, but as a whole they didn't produce a great deal of light. Pierrot went over to the ditch. Once again the woman shrieked with terror. Once again he took a few steps, and saw her. Furthermore, he made out a bike not far away.

"Mustn't be afraid," that was what he started by saying. No answer. He repeated his remark. Won over, no doubt, by the gentleness of his voice, the woman climbed out of the ditch. She came towards him, saying:

"It's idiotic, but I'm scared rigid. I've been there a couple of hours, dying of fear."

Pierrot heard Yvonne's voice. She was quite close to him now. A ray of light, arriving, tired after a thousand-year journey, from a star of the first magnitude, illuminated with some difficulty the tip of the nose of this young person. It was her all right: Yvonne.

"Have no more fear. Mademoiselle Pradonet," said he solemnly.

"Well of all the . . ." said she, struck dumb.

She examined him.

"I seem to recognize you," she said without conviction.

"I used to work at Uni Park," he said. "We even saw each other several times, you and I."

"Then we don't need to introduce ourselves," said Yvonne. "But get me out of here."

"Is that bike yours?"

"Yes. But I've got a flat tire. What's more. I'm lost."

"Me too," said Pierrot.

"That doesn't make things any better," said Yvonne. "Talk about bad luck. Well then, so you're lost?"

"Yes."

As he went to get the bike out of the ditch, he added that it didn't bother him all that much.

"Come to think of it," said Yvonne, "you're a pal of Gontran's."

"Gontran?"

"Don't you know Paradis?"

"Ah! his name's Gontran. First I heard of it. You learn something new every day."

"Well, he's a bloody idiot," said Yvonne.

"No? Why?"

He inspected Mamz'elle Pradonet's metal steed, but there wasn't much to be learnt from it. He noticed that the carrier was heavily laden.

"Were you going camping with him?" Pierrot asked.

"Congratulations," she said warmly, "you're no fool."

"One does what one can," said Pierrot rapidly.

"Yes, that was it, we left to go camping together. I told my parents that there was a whole gang of us. They didn't need me there anymore. Did you know Uni Park had been burned down?"

"Yes."

"I was entitled to a holiday, then. So I left the day before yesterday with Gontran . . . But . . . are you interested in my story?"

"Of course," said Pierrot.

"We spent the night at Saint-Mouézy-sur-Eon," she went on, "but not in the tent. We were too knackered to put it up, especially as I don't know how. I'll have to learn. Have *you* done any camping?"

"In the army."

"Don't talk rubbish. So we spent the night in a hotel in the village."

Pierrot didn't feel like asking for details.

"This morning," Yvonne went on, "we were both full of beans, we left at six, we rode up the hill at Butanges like champions, everything was going fine. Not that I'm all that keen on sports, cycling et cetera, but even so, fresh air, it has its charm, don't you think?"

"Yes," said Pierrot.

"Apart from that, we aren't going to stay here all night chatting, are we?"

"No," said Pierrot.

He suggested that they should find their way back to the hotel, looked for the Great Bear amongst the stellar chaos so as to find the north, and finally invited Yvonne to follow him "over there," without precisely knowing where. She thought he was less lost than he wanted to admit, and started walking with him. He put the bike over his shoulder, and Yvonne put some of the luggage on her back.

"Where'd I got to with my story?" asked Yvonne, after several steps in silence.

"You'd just ridden up the hill at Butanges."

"There, we left the main road, Gontran wanted to go through the forest of Palengrenon. But actually, you don't give a damn about my story."

"Me? Of course I do."

"Oh no you don't, but you can say that your Gontran is a right bastard."

"What did he do?"

"No no, you're not interested. But tell me, what the hell were you doing on this road at this hour?"

"I was going for a breather, and I got lost."

"Just like me," said Yvonne.

"Where's Paradis?" asked Pierrot.

"I don't know, and I don't want to know."

"What are you going to do now?"

"I'll get my bike repaired and carry on on my own."

"Wouldn't you like to come to Palinsac with me? I'll take you in my car."

"You've got a car?"

She was so radiant with joy that she might have been another star.

"It's only a van, but it goes," said Pierrot.

And he started telling her animal stories.

8

THE PARIS EVENING PAPERS don't reach Palinsac much before half-past eight, and sometimes not until nine. People then made a dash for the bookseller-stationer Paul's shop, especially sport lovers. After which, a few of the town's inhabitants would one by one come and buy the folio that would send them to sleep.

One of Paul's regular customers never came before nine in the evening, just as the shop was closing. He took his paper, consigned his sous to the bowl that collected the product of the clientele's honesty and then, but only sometimes, unfolded it, the paper, after which, if the fancy took him, he commented on it with some competence and not without originality.

Paul listened to him with the same reverence as he listened to the reflections of his other regulars; had he compared these various remarks and these varying appreciations he could have managed, thanks to a sound critical method, to arrive at an objective evaluation of events. But he didn't give a damn. He simply didn't. Which considerably simplified his life.

The customer took one look at the paper and exclaimed:

"Bollocks, my dear Paul! It's all bollocks! Politics, wars,

sport: totally uninteresting. What *I* get a kick out of is all the news items and court cases. That great stupid animal, Society—I don't want any truck with it. Individuals and how they behave, now that means something to me. All the rest: gammon, gas, hot air. As proved by the fact that the moment there's more than one of you in a discussion, you talk crap. It takes two to commit a murder, and the moment there's a third in a couple, someone's cuckolded. Error, crime, and adultery: that's all that makes men interesting. On a large scale it becomes ugly; on the individual level it's amusing."

There was a silence because Paul considered these remarks vaguely incoherent. They didn't disconcert him, however, for they were not unprecedented.

"And at your place," he asked calmly, "everything all right?"

"Not bad, thanks. The usual little problems of the trade. Two magnificent macaws have just died on me. and they were beginning to ride a bicycle perfectly. I was thinking of making a little tandem for them, but now they're dead. Adieu. But when they've been stuffed, I'll still get a few francs out of them. Milou, one of my monkeys, has got diarrhea; he's going to snuff it too. He was very likeable, though. A good pal. Ah well . . ."

"And what does the paper say?" asked Paul.

"It doesn't mention any of that. But here . . . look . . . there are three columns on a war . . . and next to them, two on a change of minister . . . one on a prizefight . . . one on an election to the Academy . . . All that, it's collective stuff, it stinks, it's an epidemic. I repeat, my dear Paul, for a man to be as interesting as an animal, he has to be on his own, or, at the very most, less than three—you know the beast with two backs, my dear Paul? Very singular, my dear Paul, very singular. And it's to be regretted that there aren't any stuffed ones to be seen in the museums. It has very strange habits, which have absolutely nothing to do with urbanism, hygiene, philanthropy, or common courtesy. Vroutt! vroutt! what a comic symbiosis!"

"Ah, Monsieur Voussois," said Paul, "you're a queer fish."

He echoed his own laugh. He couldn't stop.

"I'd rather make people laugh than cry," said Voussois. "I'm not such a bad fellow after all."

"Good old Monsieur Voussois. And the news items, what do they say?"

"Hang on a moment . . . What did I tell you? Just listen to this: 'HE BIT HIS RABBITS OUT OF AN EXCESS OF LOVE.' What d'you think of that? It's a chap who kept rabbits, and the society for the protection of animals is after him because he loved them so much that he tossed them up in the air and caught them in his teeth. Eh? Isn't that wonderful? It throws far more light on the way men are made than eighteen wars and thirty-six peace treaties. Doesn't it, my dear Paul?"

"I'd never be the one to contradict you," said Paul.

"Ah! and here's something else that fascinates me:

"'THE INQUIRY INTO THE CAUSES OF THE FIRE AT UNI PARK.'"

"I went there once, to Uni Park," said Paul, "after my cousin Muche's wedding. We all had paper hats and kazoos, and we went on all the rides. Talk about laugh—we certainly laughed. I can even positively state that we had fun, and I'll tell you something. Monsieur Voussois, it was odd, but it was at the Palace of Fun (so well named), it was above all at the Palace of Fun that I acquired my knowledge . . . of Parisiennes . . . Oh la la! . . . when I think about it . . ."

"Allow me to make an observation," said Voussois.

"I allow you."

"That I consider all those things idiotic, obscene, vulgar and unseemly. They only appeal to the basest instincts of man: mystification, libertinage, bullying, and rowdiness. They merit nothing but reprobation from serious people, workers and artistes. In fact, I was extremely glad to hear that all that filth had gone up in flames."

"You've already told me that."

"When I was reading the paper I could hear the fireproofed timbers crackling, and I could see the ones that weren't fireproofed blazing. A joyous sight!"

"And have they found the culprit?"

"They'll never find him. The inquiry decided that it was caused accidentally."

"Just as well," said Paul. "That makes one criminal the less."

"But it wasn't a crime to set fire to Uni Park!"

"Monsieur Voussois, Monsieur Voussois, they'd accuse you of it if you'd been in Paris that day!"

"But it's well established that I was here?"

"I was joking," said Paul, the newspaper seller.

After a little silence, Voussois repeated:

"No, it wasn't a crime to set fire to Uni Park!"

He folded his paper and put it in his pocket.

"Good night, my dear Paul. You see how interesting news items are."

"Especially when they happen in the summer."

Paul liked a laugh.

Voussois lived a little way outside the town; he wasn't often to be seen. He lived amid his animals. His domain was surrounded by high walls, no one knew what went on within, and people rarely saw the animals that were brought there or taken away. They merely heard their cries, which were varied. But all this was so discreet that, when tourists came looking for curiosities, no one in the district ever mentioned the place to them. The mayor, a man of initiative, dreamed of organizing excursions ending up at the Training Institute; at the station, monkeys would be punching the tickets, elephants transporting the luggage, camels carrying the passengers. In the restaurants, porcupines would be offering their toothpicks, and kangaroos would be carrying telegrams in their pouches (or marsupia). But all this was only a dream, which the mayor would not have dared mention to that Monsieur Voussois, a difficult man who had his own ideas.

From the bottom of the garden, Voussois saw a light in the dining room; someone was waiting for him. As he thought he knew who that someone was, Voussois took the time to say good night to his animals, stroking muzzles, patting spines or flanks, distributing tidbits. Milou was trembling with fever under his blankets; his cage smelled particularly unpleasant because of his squitters; he offered Voussois a delicate little hand, now flabby and abandoned. Voussois said some encouraging words to him very softly, but he knew very well that the poor beast was going to croak. Milou shut his eyes and took his hand back.

In the dining room, the man waiting for him had had himself brought the remains of the dinner and was stowing it away voraciously. He waved his knife, from which a filament of meat was suspended: this was to say hello. Voussois sat down opposite him and poured himself a glass of wine.

"Well," he asked, "did you see the damage?"

"Yes," the visitor replied, scattering fragments of cold veal with his mouth. "'S'nothing left."

"Why didn't you write to me?"

"Couldn't be bothered."

"And the tomb?"

"Intact."

"Really? There's nothing left of Uni Park, but the tomb is safe and sound?"

"Correct. I saw it."

Voussois rubbed his hands in jubilation. He waited until his visitor had finished shoveling in the grub, and then asked him:

"Tell me about it."

"Well, just imagine everything smashed to bits, but blackened, twisted, melted. The chairoplane tower, the Alpinic Railway, they're just old iron. But you've read the papers, haven't you?"

"Yes. Then that's really the way it is?"

"I've already told you so."

"Because the papers, you know, they make things up, I know them."

"In ruins, that's what it is. In ruins."

"And now?"

"Well, I had a chat with Pradonet, after the 'catastrophe,' as he calls it. He wants to build a gigantic palace on the site, make a fairground seven storeys high, not counting a parachute tower he wants to erect on the roof. You can see how ambitious he is. Just one snag—the tomb. He wants to buy the land and demolish the chapel, but there's nothing doing: Mounnezergues won't sell."

"That's good. And what does old Pradonet say about it?"

"It makes him sad."

They both laughed, and began to smoke cigarettes and drink little glasses.

"By the way," said the visitor, "someone recognized me as being Jojo Mouilleminche's brother."

"No?"

"Yes. I was told something like this: I recognize the way you talk, you wouldn't by any chance be from—hang on, from Houilles, and therefore the brother of Jojo Mouilleminche, would you?"

"And what did you answer?"

"What did you expect me to answer? I answered: yes."

"And who was it who asked you that?"

"The widow Prouillot."

"Did she know Jojo Mouilleminche?"

"Yes. She'd been his mistress."

"The widow Prouillot?"

"Yes. In those days, she was dancing in a nightclub."

"In those days. What days?"

"Something like twenty years ago."

"About twenty years?"

Voissois considered the matter at length.

"I don't remember her."

He inspected everything in him that could be situated more or less in that period and tried to exhume some mistresses from it. Covered in the ashes of the varied colors of the seasons, try as he would, he couldn't manage to discover amongst them a Léonie who used to shake a leg in a honky-tonk.

"I don't remember," he repeated.

"*She* remembers all right, and even though you chucked her without warning . . ."

"These things happen," said Voussois.

". . . She's kept a great big place for you in her heart. She comes over all emotional when she talks about you."

"That's all the same to me."

"Do you really not remember?"

"You know, it must have been about the time when I fell off my horse. That whole period's a bit of a blur in my mind. Maybe she was my girlfriend at the time of my accident, and maybe, also, that was the reason I chucked her: without meaning to. But as I'd have left her one day or another, a bit sooner, a bit later . . ."

"In any case," said Crouïa Bey, "she cried a lot when I told her of your death."

"Which one?"

"One I invented. Believe it or not, you died ten years later in romantic fashion, trying to climb over a wall to get to a girl you loved."

"Did she like it, that end to my existence?"

"Yes. But the girl, that's what worries her now. She's dying to know who she was."

"Didn't you tell her?"

"No. I couldn't think of anyone. And anyway, I wasn't in Europe at the time. I told her a bit about my journeys in Africa."

"So she's still got a thing about me?"

"Precisely."

Voussois once again began to reconsider his former amours but could still find no place for a Léonie X who used to kick up her heels in a gaff.

"In any case," said Crouïa Bey, "*I'm* going to bed."

"Did your shows go well?"

"Yes. Very well. I'm knackered. I'm going to bed."

"Good night," said Voussois.

And he could still find no way to conjure up the memory of a little Léonie who used to hoof it in a café-concert. He vaguely remembered having been a little in love with a Lili who danced in the Boite a Dix Sous near the République, but with a Léonie, no.

He sat dreaming for some time, smoking and drinking little glasses. From time to time a night bird hooted. He bred them for his pleasure. He didn't try to train them. He knew each one's voice. He would have liked them, when he was dead, to come and nest by his tomb. And he was just about to start thinking about Uni Park again when the doorbell rings. He stands up and sees through the open window a van parked outside the iron gate.

He went up to it.

The light over the entrance lit up the MAMAR, in big letters, decorating the van. Voussois was expecting it: Psermis had written to him.

"This is no time." he said to the driver.

"A thousand apologies," said Pierrot, "I'd certainly have waited until tomorrow morning, but all things considered I'd rather get things sorted out this evening. I have to get rid of Mésange. Believe it or not, he wants to rape my fiancée! I had to knock him out. He's in the car, tied up. What's more, he'd got fed up with me wearing glasses. Things were getting nasty."

"I don't give a sod about your fiancée," said Voussois. "That was no reason to beat up my livestock."

"That's arguable," said Pierrot.

"And Pistolet?"

"Oh! *he's* a good little chap. He's asleep. The rest of the cargo behaved well. You'll see: I took good care of them. And I assure you, I haven't damaged Mésange. Just a nice little tap on the crumpet with a stick. And apart from the passion that came over him, we hit it off fine, him and me."

"But your fiancée, where is she?"

"You're very inquisitive," Pierrot remarked.

"And you seem to me to be a queer specimen. You could easily have waited until tomorrow morning, in spite of your cock-and-bull stories. Still, bring your car in."

Pierrot got back into his seat and Voussois opened the gates for him.

Then they unloaded the van. The parrots began to squawk, and the ones that could talk brought their knowledge of human abusive language into full play. Some of their colleagues, *en pension* with Voussois, answered them, as did other beasts. All hell was let loose. Pistolet, woken by the tumult, recognized Voussois and went and said hello to him. Of his own accord he found somewhere to spend the night. Mésange was still semi-conscious; Voussois revived him. They shook hands tenderly. Deeply moved by all his adventures, Mésange raised no objections to bedding down in a cage that seemed familiar to him. Pierrot was cowering in a corner to prevent the sight of him once again exciting the fury of his traveling companion.

When all this work had been completed, Voussois invited Pierrot to have a drink with him before going off to bed. They went into the dining room. The table hadn't been quite cleared. There were wine and liqueur stains on the cloth. The window was open on to the park. The animals had calmed down and were going back to sleep, except for the favorite screech owls, who sang from time to time. The two men sat down facing one another. Pierrot had the vague impression that he'd already met this chap somewhere.

"Did it take you long to get here?" asked Voussois.

"I left the day before yesterday," Pierrot replied. "I spent the night at Saint-Flers-sur-Cavaillet, and I got here this evening. Their van's just an old heap, you know."

"Have you known Psermis long?"

"About a week."

"Is that all? But how long have you been with the Mamar Circus?"

"About a week. When people ask me a question like that, that's usually the answer I have to give. I never stay much longer in the joints I work in. It isn't that I like change, it just happens that way. Before, for example, I was at Uni Park. Well, I stayed there two days in all, and not even two days running."

"Didn't it burn down, that Uni Park?"

"And how. And what a blaze! I didn't see it, but I can

imagine it, judging by the little that was left of it, of Uni Park. Smoking ruins, Monsieur. It was really something. I was on the spot the same morning. Incidentally, it was that day that I met Monsieur Psermis. And anyway, he was somewhat talking through his hat on the subject. He claimed he'd seen how it happened: planes in flames, he said, that came away from the tower and set fire to the four corners of Uni Park. It's crazy, isn't it? The papers say it was an accident; you have to believe them: what do you think about it, Monsieur Voussois?"

"I couldn't care less," said Voussois.

"Me neither," replied Pierrot

"And what on earth was he doing in those parts, Psermis?"

"Mamar has set up on the site opposite Uni Park. You must know that"

"Really?"

"I think so."

"Well, let's come back to Mésange for a moment. You could have done him in, you know."

"I'm really sorry. The whole of the first part of the trip, everything was just fine. Monsieur Psermis had warned me that he wasn't easy. Yet we'd become buddies. But there you are, I met my fiancée . . ."

"Ah!"

"Yes. You find that surprising? It's the truth, though. She was going camping around here with a girlfriend, and believe it or not she bashed up her bike. I picked her up on the road where it happened. Wouldn't you have done the same?"

"Yes."

"There: you see. At first, everything went very well. Yvonne—that's my fiancée—was nice to him, and he was amiable with her. I won't tell you in detail how things went wrong, but just before we got here he passed from indecency to obscenity. He was becoming dangerous. What's more, he tried to pull my specs off. I didn't like it. Finally, he threw himself on Yvonne. You can imagine how frightened she was. So I knocked him out, your Mésange. and knocked him out good. Poor old chap."

"Do you like animals?" Voussois asked.

"I think so. But I've never seen so many, and at such close quarters, as in the last forty-eight hours."

"I hope you'll take good care of the ones you're going to take back to Paris."

"Three dogs, twenty ducks, a sea lion, and a secretary bird, that's what they told me."

"Correct. Have you ever seen one, a secretary bird?"

"No. But Monsieur Psermis explained what they are."

"And what will you do after that? Have you got a job with the Mamar Circus?"

"No. Just for this one little trip. After that, I don't know. I'll look around. A new trade doesn't frighten me. But I wouldn't want to be a clown or a freak. Acrobat, now, I'd have quite liked that. Tightrope walker: terrific. But I'm boring you, talking about myself. Excuse me. It's time to go to bed."

He drained his glass and stood up. As did, shortly afterwards, Voussois, who asked him:

"Would you be interested in working here with me? Acclimatization. Breeding. Training. It's a profession you could stay in all your life. And it's interesting. It's an opportunity for you, or better still: a stroke of luck. I need someone at the moment. Think it over."

"Thank you very much," said Pierrot.

"And you'll be back tomorrow?"

"I will. Monsieur Voussois."

They went out. Voussois went to open the entrance gate.

"Don't bother," said Pierrot. "If you don't mind, I'll leave the van with you. It'll save me paying for a garage."

"I don't mind," said Voussois. "Good night. And I hope your fiancée won't be afraid of the wicked satyr any longer."

"I hope so too," said Pierrot solemnly. "Good night. Monsieur Voussois."

It took him a good ten minutes to get back to the town center and the Hôtel de l'Arche, where he had reserved a room. So he had plenty of time to think over the proposition Voussois had just made him, but he didn't need that long to make up his mind because he'd already done so. So he would teach monkeys to put on evening dress, dogs to turn backward somersaults, and sea lions to applaud themselves for their clever tricks. Perhaps he might even manage to teach a cat the fine art of playing the drum, and a lion the noble sport of roller skating. In any case, he felt full of sympathy for every species of animal, and willing to feed and groom them, each according to its species. Having thus (momentarily) decided on his future, his heart felt less heavy and hence more capable of giving itself up to some of the other preoccupations weighing it down, this heart that he had just liberated.

However much in love with Yvonne he was, he had nevertheless not blinded himself to the point of not noticing that she hadn't the slightest desire to sleep with him, even out of pure goodness of heart; furthermore, it was quite obvious that she didn't love him. That was the way it was, and not otherwise. As proved by the enthusiasm with which she had agreed to share the room of her sinistromanual stepmother, met by chance in a street in the town, looking for a hotel. Pierrot had therefore had to content himself with a hermit's room. To pass the time, he had driven the animals to their owner, especially as, since he had clobbered Mésange, he was not without anxiety about his state of health. As for what she had come to do in Palinsac, Yvonne's sinistromanual stepmother, she hadn't said.

Pierrot had reached this point in his thoughts as he entered the little town, and the twelve strokes of midnight were just oozing from a thirteenth-century belfry. A cat crossed the still-deserted street; it was often grey, and it vanished rapidly, full of distrust at the sight of this passerby.

Pierrot made a detour and passed the station, where he was hoping to find some animation; he wasn't looking forward to shutting himself in behind the morose door of a room in which the desired companion was not awaiting him. But the trains had all already gone or come, and the railmen weren't expecting any others until the first blush of morn. Everything was now asleep, and the only people who might still be awake were perhaps a signalman or a telegraph operator who cared little about giving this part of the town the picturesque physiognomy Pierrot demanded of it. The surrounding cafés had long since put their chairs to bed on their marble tables, chairs tenderly polished by behinds that cared little about journeys.

Pierrot walked slowly back to his hotel. He could hear his own footsteps.

The night porter came to let him in. He was wearing braces.

"Good evening," said Pierrot. "I could do with a drink."

"Difficult," said the fellow. "The bar's closed. That doesn't matter, though, I'll find you some liquid somewhere. I wouldn't refuse a dog a glass of water."

"I rather fancy a white wine."

"Follow me."

He switched on the light in the deserted café, where the furniture was asleep. It had been swept but the early morning sawdust was lacking.

"Well then: do I give you a white wine?" the night porter asked.

"Yes, I'd like one," said Pierrot, looking absentmindedly at a minute object somewhere in the picture.

"Monsieur looks dreamy," said the night porter.

"That's not my style," said Pierrot. "Although I often find myself thinking of nothing."

"That's already better than not thinking at all," said the night porter. "Is it good, my white wine?"

"No worse than any other."

"When people see people of your age looking the way you do, they usually say they've got love trouble."

"You think so? It's true for me: in the present case. That's the strangest thing."

"Are you very unhappy?"

"Oh yes! Very. Naturally, I can't measure how much for you."

"No, of course not. Me too, I used to suffer in the olden days. It hurts, doesn't it?"

The telephone rang. The porter went to it, spoke to it, came back.

"It's," said he, "the two ladies in number 15 wanting a couple of lemon squashes."

"Make a third one for me," said Pierrot, "and I'll take them up."

"You can't do that!"

Pierrot estimates the night porter's conscience at a hundred sous, and that's what he tips him; hence, he was able to take the required beverages up to the ladies in number 15. He stopped outside the door and listened: they were chatting. He tapped, he was told to come in, which he did.

Yvonne was already in bed. Madame Léonie Prouillot, enveloped in a Sino-Japanese kimono, was sitting in an armchair with her legs crossed and smoking a cigarillo.

"Well!" said Léonie, "what's got into you? Have you got a job as night porter here?"

"Oh no!"

He distributed the refreshments and put his glass down on a little table, by which he then sat.

"Have you got rid of your animals?" Yvonne asked.

"Yes. I'm going to fetch the others tomorrow."

Léonie examined him.

"What sort of an education have you had?"

Pierrot gave her an uncordial look.

"I'm no more of a moron than the next person," he replied.

Ignoring this piece of impertinence, Léonie continued her interrogation:

"Do you know Petit-Pouce?"

"The Uni Park one? Of course."

"And what sort of a fellow is he?"

"He is someone," said Pierrot, "to whom you entrusted a confidential mission."

"How do you know that?" Léonie exclaimed.

She was taken aback.

"I've already told you," Pierrot retorted, "that I'm no more of a moron than the next person. Come on, make a clean breast of it!"

"Go on, tell him about your old amours," said Yvonne, amazed at Pierrot's sudden intelligence.

"Listen," said Léonie to Pierrot, "I'm not giving away any secrets. But this is what's on my mind: I want to know what became of a girl who, about ten years ago, was the cause of a tragic death. It happened here, in Palinsac. Petit-Pouce was supposed to find this girl for me. I advanced him some cash to do that. He left about a week ago; my goodness, it was the day before the fire. Forty-eight hours later he sent me a telegram saying he was leaving for Saint-Mouézy-sur-Eon, where he was hoping to find her. Since then, no news; and I'd given him a week, no more, for that little expedition. As I realized he'd conned me, I came here to make my own inquiries. You might be able to help me. I'd pay for your hotel and meals, and give you ten francs pocket money."

"I have to go back to Paris tomorrow," said Pierrot. "I'm extremely sorry, Madame."

"Oh, forget your beastly animals."

"No, Madame."

He drank some of his lemon squash; he found it quite disgusting.

"Well, all right," said Léonie, "but then there was no point in making me come out with all this."

"She doesn't want to tell you," said Yvonne to Pierrot, "that the guy who got killed, she was in love with him. And he chucked her, ten years before."

"But," Pierrot suddenly asked Léonie, "why are you only taking an interest in it now?"

"Because I only heard about it a few days ago," Léonie replied.

"The fakir told her," said Yvonne. "Crouïa Bey."

"Did he tell her fortune?" Pierrot asked.

"Of course not! He's the brother of the chap in question."

"What a carry-on," said Pierrot coldly.

"And it's all ancient history," said Léonie. "Twenty years, do you realize what that is, you young people?"

"It's more or less the number of years between me and my first communion," said Pierrot.

"No kidding," said Yvonne, "you look young. No one would think it."

"Are you really thirty?" Léonie asked.

"Well, twenty-eight," Pierrot replied.

But Léonie wasn't interested in Pierrot's age.

"Tomorrow," she said, "I'm going to start my investigation. And you," she asked Yvonne, "what are you going to do?"

"I'll stay with you two or three days to see how you go about it. If you don't mind. After that, I'll carry on with my travels. I don't know what became of my friends."

"Me," said Pierrot, "I'm leaving tomorrow."

"With your livestock?" asked Yvonne.

"Yes. This time I think I'm going to have a sea lion and a secretary bird."

"The little wild boar was very sweet," said Yvonne, "but the ape, what a swine!"

"Nothing happened between you, did it?" Léonie suddenly asked.

"Between who?" asked Yvonne. "Between the ape and me?"

"Of course not, idiot. Between you and Pierrot."

"Oh no, Madame!" said Pierrot.

He blushed.

"Shall we see you tomorrow?" Léonie asked him.

"I'd like to. Shall we have an aperitif together?"

"All right."

"And give my proposition some more thought," said Léonie.

The next morning, Pierrot went to see Voussois, but he found only Urbain, one of the employees, who told him to come back at two when everything would be ready for him. He showed him round the Park and introduced him not only to the subjects he was to take back to Paris, namely the three dogs, Fifi, Mimi, and Titi, all of them fox terriers capable of doing backward somersaults, of presenting arms, and of adding up two-figure numbers if they were given enough help; the twenty ducks trained to run around in a circle and swim through the little ponds they found in their path; the sea lion, that juggled, as was only right and proper, although in other respects it was of below-average intelligence and mainly desirous of consuming great quantities of fish (Pierrot would be provided with an ample supply of these comestibles for the journey), and incidentally they called this sea lion Mizzy; and finally Marcel, the secretary bird, a great strapping creature with three feathers, especially brought over from Abyssinia to pacify the poultry yards; and also the other animals Voussois was still training and the ones he hadn't been able to train, and the ones he had no intention of training but in which he nevertheless traded or which he acclimatized simply for love of the art or out of pure sympathy. Pierrot also caught sight of someone lying on a chaise longue—Crouïa Bey—who was sunbathing. He recognized him perfectly and was amazed. He questioned the servant and was told that that was Monsieur Voussois's brother, a professional trapper and distinguished catcher of wild animals, and that he had traveled in many countries. Pierrot didn't insist.

He spent his morning there, and thought it must be pretty pleasant to live among all these animals. He was more and more resolved to accept Voussois's offer, but he didn't wait any longer for him when he saw the first stroke of noon coming up.

At the café which occupied the ground floor of his hotel, he found Yvonne and Léonie, drinking vermouths-cassis and fanning themselves. He ordered one as well, put a big chunk of ice in his glass and watched it melt.

"And your inquiry, Madame Pradonet," he asked Léonie, "coming along nicely, is it?"

"I haven't had time to do a lot," she replied. "I went to the town hall, but they couldn't find any trace of the death of anyone called Mouilleminche. The town clerk, who's an old

Palinsacois, has never heard of a death like his. Nor at the local paper: I went there."

"It's odd," said Pierrot.

"Don't you think so?"

"Yes, I do. It doesn't look easy."

"No. And naturally, in both places they told me that someone had already been to see them and asked the same questions."

Petit-Pouce, thus conjured up, immediately manifested himself in the form of a telegram brought by the hotel porter.

"It's been forwarded from Paris," said Léonie. "Good lord, this is odd. Just listen to this: 'Am on the right track. Please send another thousand francs. Poste restante, Saint-Mouézy-sur-Eon.' It's signed Petit-Pouce."

"He's been smarter than you," said Yvonne.

"I'll go and send him his thousand francs this minute," said Léonie enthusiastically.

"The post office will be closed," Pierrot remarked.

"So it will," said Léonie, and she sat down again.

"Saint-Mouézy-sur-Eon?" said Pierrot, giving the matter some thought. "But I came through there on my way here . . ."

"Of course," said Yvonne, "it's on the Route Nationale Xbis. I came through there too."

"So you did," said Pierrot coldly.

Yvonne looks at him curiously. He didn't flinch.

"I wonder what on earth he can have discovered," said Léonie, who is learning Petit-Pouce's telegram by heart.

She's dreaming.

"You know," said Pierrot, so as not to let the conversation die completely, "I met someone we know at Voussois's this morning. I was a little amazed to see him there."

"Ah!" said the two women.

"You'll never guess who."

"Gontran!" exclaimed Yvonne.

And in fact, Paradis was getting off his bicycle right in front of them.

"He's one of my camping pals," said Yvonne to Léonie. "He's found me."

Paradis, extremely surprised to see Pierrot and the boss's wife there, didn't quite dare to move.

"Come on over," Yvonne called to him.

He came up.

"Where are our pals?" she asked him.

"What pals?" he asked in return.

He was still somewhat flabbergasted.

"Idiot. The friends we were camping with."

"Ah yes!" he said, "ah yes! They're waiting for us."

"Come and have a drink with us," Léonie quickly suggested.

Pierrot and he shook hands.

"I didn't expect to find you here," said Paradis.

"You meet everyone here," said Pierrot.

"Except the girl I'm looking for," said Léonie. "And who may have five children by now."

"That would be pretty amazing," said Pierrot.

Then he saw Voussois coming up to them.

A few seconds later, Léonie fell fainting in his arms.

Epilogue

THAT MORNING IT WAS SUNDAY, and the inauguration of the Chaillot Zoophilic Gardens. As soon as he was awake, Pierrot remembered that he had decided to go and see the opening of the Voussois Park which, on the site of the defunct and incinerated Uni Park, offered a thousand rare or strange animals to the public eye, a year, almost day for day, after the fire that had destroyed the booths and rides that Pradonet had formerly brought together for the pleasure of provincials, toughs, and philosophers.

It took Pierrot some time to decide to get up; he was becoming a sluggard with age. He could hear the hymns slowly evaporating from the convent. A neighbor switched on a radio full blast. Down in the street, the peaceful hum of cars. The sun begins to crawl along the balcony.

When he was out of bed, Pierrot made a perfunctory toilet and went down to have his coffee, which he laced, a habit he'd got into. Then he went back up to his room. As, on the other hand, he didn't play the horses anymore, and, as a consequence, didn't buy *La Veine* anymore, he now put his feet on the bedspread, which he was wearing out. He smoked two or three cigarettes, dozed, and conjured up a few memories.

He passed under review the individuals he had known at
the time of Uni Park; there were some whose names he had
already forgotten; the only one he remembered clearly was
Mounnezergues, a likeable character whose heir he might have
become . . . if, that is, you could believe old Mounnezergues's
tales. Pierrot had never been back to see him, not even to
thank him for having got him a little trip at the expense of
the Mamar Circus; after that he'd found a job on the other
side of Paris; and Yvonne was no longer to be seen in the
Porte-d'Argenteuil district, she had fallen into dissolute ways
in waterproof tents that sheltered her from excessively blue
skies. As for Voussois, Pierrot had decided, after all, that training and caging animals didn't appeal to him.

A sort of current had carried him far away from those
chance encounters which life didn't intend him to become
attached to. It had been one of the most rounded, the most
complete, the most autonomous episodes of his life, and when
he thought of it with all the requisite concentration (which
anyway only rarely happened to him), he saw clearly how all
its constituent elements could have been combined into an
adventure that might have developed into a mystery, later to
be solved like a problem in algebra in which there are as many
equations as there are unknowns, and he saw how it had not
turned out like that. He saw too the novel it could have made,
a detective novel with a crime, a guilty party and a detective,
and the requisite interplay between the different asperities of
the demonstration, and he saw the novel that it *had* become, a
novel so shorn of artifice that it was quite impossible to know
whether it contained a riddle to be solved or whether it did
not, a novel in which everything might have been interlinked
according to police plans but which was in fact totally depleted

of all the pleasures provided by an entertainment, an activity of that order.

Pierrot wiped the lenses of his cheaters, looked at the time on a turnip, stubbed out the embers of his cigarette on the marble top of his bedside cupboard, whose pot he immediately thereafter utilized, even though it was nearly midday. He went and had an aperitif at a small café whose tranquil terrace formed a right angle at the corner of two streets. Then he lunched in a restaurant, also small, almost as small as the cafe. And then he slowly, calmly, made his way to the Porte d'Argenteuil. He passed trine families in their Sunday best, soldiers on leave, little maidservants far from their dusters and stoves. He stopped in front of the shops: he still liked them. Automobiles, velocipedes, postage stamps, he examined them all with the severity of the connoisseur untrammeled by all the worries of possession, but with the satisfaction afforded by this disinterestedness. He passed the ball-bearings shop and had the pleasure of once again seeing the little steel spheres still describing their impeccable trajectories.

He was approaching the Porte de Chaillot. There was a kind of fog over in that direction: it was a crowd of people trampling the asphalt or pulverizing the gravel. They were lining up to gain entrance to the Zoophilic Park. Pierrot looked at this mob in disgust and had no wish to mingle with it. And while he was completing his general survey by an inspection of the pavement on which he had remained, he caught sight of a man leaning against a lamppost whom he thought he recognized. He passed him, walked around him, stared at him, and addressed him.

"Good afternoon, Monsieur Pradonet," were the words subsequent to this examination.

"Good afternoon, Monsieur," said Pradonet in a soft voice.

"Don't you recognize me?" Pierrot asked.

"My goodness, no," Pradonet replied, in a benign tone of voice, "I can't place you. You mustn't be offended, but I've met so many people in my life . . ."

"I understand. And anyway, you probably only saw me two or three times. I used to work at Uni Park . . ."

"Ah! . . . Uni Park . . ." Pradonet sighed.

"Not for long, it's true. Don't you remember, one day I played a trick on you . . . you fell backwards into a bumper car . . ."

"Ah!" Pradonet exclaimed happily, "*do* I remember! You had me, that day. But I had my revenge the next day: I had you sacked because you were chatting up my daughter Yvonne. Ah! those were the days!"

"Shall we go and have a drink?"

"No thanks. My liver's playing up, and Vichy-fraise makes me puke. Let's walk a bit, we can talk."

He led him over to the Avenue de la Porte d'Argenteuil, and they made their way towards the Seine. At first, Pradonet said nothing.

"And Mademoiselle Yvonne?" Pierrot asked, barely breathing.

"She's married to one of your former pals, I think, a fellow called Paradis."

"Oh! Really?"

"Bit of a shock, is it?" Pradonet asked. "You were badly smitten, eh? Pah! there were so many of them, you know, there were so many of them . . . You want to see her? Well, over there, at that paybox, that's her. Because she deserted me and went to work for Voussois."

Pierrot pretended to look, but he didn't want to see. There was indeed a kind of sentry box in front of which some good people were jostling one another. He focused his eyes on something else, somewhere else, above, yes, over there, a leaf on a tree at the very end of a branch, that one rather than another . . .

Over the walls of the Zoophilic Park, over the heads of the sightseers, wafted the roar of a lion, followed by the trumpeting of an elephant. Various birds sang, each in its own language.

"Yes," Pradonet resumed, "those were the days."

As they were passing the corner of the Rue des Larmes, Pierrot said nothing.

"I don't know, though," Pradonet went on, "why I should tell you all my woes. It's too long a story. In a word, let me just tell you that they threw me out. Who's 'they'? Madame Prouillot, who was living with me, and Monsieur Voussois, the animal trainer that she met again, on information she got from a fakir, in a little provincial town. Yes, Monsieur, he'd chucked her twenty years before, and twenty years later he comes back to pluck her like a flower. After which these two lovebirds, so full of constancy, have nothing better to do than concoct a sinister financial, legal, and commercial scheme to prevent every possibility of my creating a new and more splendid Uni Park, in which they are morally supported, yes Monsieur, and sustained by the ill-omened, yes Monsieur, fateful and prodigiously singular presence of a Poldevian chapel in which there repose the bones of a certain Prince Luigi."

"I met you one day at Monsieur Mounnezergues's house," said Pierrot, to show that the conversation interested him.

"Did you know him?" Pradonet asked politely.

"A little."

"How odd," said Pradonet. "And the tomb, did you know that too, then?"

"And how," Pierrot replied.

"And what about me then," Pradonet wailed, "do *I* know it! . . . If it hadn't been there I'd have built a Palace of Fun on that site the like of which doesn't exist anywhere in the world. Ah! what good times we'd have had! from top to bottom of the seven floors I'd planned. You'd have been able to find every game there, every novelty, every practical joke, every attraction, every pastime . . . From one end of the year to the other, and from the middle of the day until the middle of the night, the crowds would have come flocking in, there'd have been infinite excitement provoking either laughter or lubricity. These crowds would have been shrieking with joy and making such a rumpus that not even the thunder of my loud speakers would have been able to drown it . . . And a Poldevian prince had to come and die on the very selfsame spot twenty years earlier! And a wax-molder had to dedicate himself to the peace of his ashes! That chapel, Monsieur, was a mine dug under my castles in Spain. Crash bang wallop, one vile day everything blew up. I was defenseless against the deadly plots of my perfidious adversary. And since I couldn't achieve in its full perfection this Babylonian edifice I wanted to create, well then, God damn and blast it, let everything be fucked up, let Voussois marry the widow Prouillot, and let him anchor his benign Noah's Ark on the charred ground of what was once Uni Park. I didn't even want to resist, no Monsieur, I didn't even want to . . . Ah, Monsieur! ah, Monsieur! ah! . . . That Voussois, he wasn't nice to me . . . He upset me terribly . . . Ah, Monsieur, ah! . . ."

He opened his mouth two or three times without uttering a sound, like a fish expiring at the bottom of a boat, and then produced a kind of long, moaning sound and collapsed in Pierrot's arms, sobbing very loudly. Pierrot had to hold him like that for a few instants before he calmed down; after that they walked in silence up to the Rue du Pont, and there they parted.

"I'm almost there," said Pradonet, fairly calmly. "I live in this street now, with my wife, my lawful one. But all these little stories can't be of much interest to you and it is very good of you. Monsieur, to have agreed to listen so long to the maunderings of a muttonhead. Goodbye, Monsieur, and thank you."

There was a hearty handshake, and Pierrot now saw nothing in the deserted street but Pradonet's back as he slowly made his way towards his newly-found wife's little general store, and Pierrot then turned his steps towards Paris, and, as he was once again passing the Rue des Larmes, he turned down it. The chapel still existed, shrouded in just as much oblivion, just as much discretion. The framework of the Alpinic Railway no longer obumbrated it. Its neighborhood now consisted of a few rocks, and even from the street a few dog-faced baboons could sometimes be seen running about on them. Pierrot remembered his friend Mésange who, confined behind solid bars, must no doubt be bringing joy to the hearts of chatty primates, dressed in a smart suit or in short pants.

The house opposite hadn't changed in any way. Pierrot remembered his friend Mounnezergues whom he hadn't seen for a good long time. He looked at the little square surrounding Prince Luigi's tomb and he had the impression that it was less well kept (cared for) than before. He immediately crosses the road and rings at Mounnezergues's door, but the bell didn't ring. He began to walk away. He went a few steps, and then retraces them. Rings again; again silence. But he, Pierrot, understood that if he was to play his part in this story to the end, he had to go further, and go in.

Which he did.

Because the gate was not locked. He noticed that the bell

had been disconnected. As the house was parallel to the garden and its front door was in the middle, Pierrot passed in front of one of the ground floor windows. It was open: on the other side, Mounnezergues was dozing in a wicker armchair. Pierrot had been watching him sleeping for a few moments when it suddenly occurred to him that Mounnezergues was at that very moment departing this life. Panic-stricken, he shouted: "Monsieur Mounnezergues! Monsieur Mounnezergues!" And Monsieur Mounnezergues opened his eyes, recognized Pierrot, and smiled. It took him a little time to get enough strength together to open his mouth, and still longer to manage to utter a few sounds.

"Is it really you," he murmured, "are you really the young man who came to see me several times last year?"

"Yes, Monsieur."

"You went to Palinsac to return the animals Psermis wouldn't take?"

"That's right."

"Why didn't you ever come to see me again? I liked you."

"I found work on the other side of Paris; and then, I had my reasons for not coming back to this district. It reminded me of things."

"A broken heart?"

"Yes, Monsieur. It was Pradonet's daughter."

"Ah! . . . Pradonet . . ."

Pause.

"I've just seen him again," said Pierrot.

"Did he tell you his troubles?" Mounnezergues asked.

"Yes, Monsieur. And how Voussois had done him out of his Uni Park. And how . . ."

"I know, I know," Mounnezergues interrupted.

"He doesn't seem to hold it against you."

"I know. As you can well imagine. I've seen him since."

He smiled.

"Now," he said, "Prince Luigi's last sleep will no longer be disturbed by the witches' sabbath of Uni Park, the obscene pandemonium of its loud speakers, the repugnant ruckus of its so-called attractions. I die happy."

He closed his eyes for a few moments.

"Come in, though," he went on, "and give me something to write with."

"Yes, Monsieur."

Pierrot goes in and gives him something to write with; he had to search for these implements amongst a jumble of objects. Mounnezergues's house was becoming a slum. The old man sensed Pierrot's thoughts.

"I live absolutely alone," he said. "Be sure not to forget that, it's very important for what comes next."

Pierrot puts a table in front of Mounnezergues, with pen, ink, paper, blotting paper.

"This," said Mounnezergues as he wrote, "this isn't my will. My will has already been made and deposited with a lawyer. This is a codicil. I'm making you my heir. But I don't even know your name."

"Pierrot," Pierrot told him.

"Naturally," said Mounnezergues, "you will only come into this inheritance on one condition: that you replace me here and become the guardian of the chapel."

"Yes, Monsieur."

"And you must make sure that my funeral is conducted according to the instructions I'm leaving. I warn you here and now that I want to be buried by the side of the Poldevian princes I have served so well. You must make it your business to get permission from the Paris municipal authorities. You must take this letter to my lawyer tomorrow. The address is on it"

"Very well. Monsieur."

He didn't want to hurt him.

"You can leave me now," said Mounnezergues.

"But . . ." said Pierrot.

"No no, I don't need anyone. Just shut that window and come back tomorrow or the next day to see if I'm dead. I'd just as soon be alone when I enact that transformation. Adieu, my young friend, and thank you."

Pierrot shook his hand, a hand already without consistency, and withdrew, shutting the doors gently behind him.

There were slightly fewer people outside the Zoophilic Park, but Pierrot no longer had the slightest desire to go in. He didn't even want to repass the box where Yvonne worked. He preferred to go to the movies.

The next day, when he was thinking of taking Mounnezergues's letter to the lawyer, he realized that he had lost it; or rather, that he'd left it behind at Mounnezergues's house. Probably. At all events, the codicil had got lost somewhere. Pierrot was reluctant to go back that same day to see Mounnezergues who, if he was still alive, might perhaps consider this haste to certify his death somewhat indecent; and also, if he'd found the letter, reproach him for his negligence.

So Pierrot didn't go until the Tuesday. He tried to open the gate. But it was shut. He pulled on the bell, which rang. So it had been reconnected? Better still, someone came to open the gate.

"Excuse me, Madame," said Pierrot.

He stopped short It was Yvonne. He resumed, with an amiable smile:

"I believe, Madame, that we have already met. Do you

remember Palinsac and Saint-Mouézy-sur-Eon?"

"Ah! but of course . . . You were the driver of the van that picked me up on the road?"

"Precisely."

"Delighted to see you again. Monsieur . . . Monsieur. . . what was the name?"

"Pierrot."

"And what can I do for you, Monsieur Pierrot?"

"I came to inquire after Monsieur Mounnezergues."

"Monsieur Mounnezergues?" Yvonne exclaimed. "Monsieur Mounnezergues? You know him, then?"

"Yes, Madame."

"Well, the thing is, he's gone to the country to convalesce. He hasn't been very well recently. Would you like me to give him a message from you?"

Even though Yvonne was keeping the gate half-closed, Pierrot managed to get a glimpse of the garden, where a lot of comings and goings suggested a total clearance of the decks. And in two big dustbins not yet collected by the dustmen, he caught sight of broken knickknacks, odds and ends in bits and pieces, and in one, even, a wax hand. Yvonne was wearing the respectable housewife's turban around her head. And she was asking him whether he wanted to leave a message for Mounnezergues.

"Well . . . no," he said.

He looked around him. The chapel was turning gold in the sunlight and the little square was softly rustling. An animal grunted on the other side of the wall. The towing truck from the garage on the corner—where the Café Posidon had been!— was bringing in a bashed-up sports car. On Mounnezergues's house, the shutters over the windows opening on to the street were aggressively closed.

"Well . . . no" Pierrot repeated.

"Come back a bit later," said Yvonne. "In a month, two months"

"I'll do that," said Pierrot. "I'll do that. Goodbye, Madame."

"Goodbye, Monsieur Pierrot. I'll tell Monsieur Mounne-zergues that you came to inquire after him."

"You do that," said Pierrot. "Goodbye, Madame."

She shut the gate.

After a last look at the two dustbins, Pierrot departed.

When he got to the corner of the street, he stopped. He burst out laughing.